RIVAL OCEAN DIVERS

RIVAL OCEAN DIVERS

Or, The Search for a Sunken Treasure

ROY ROCKWOOD

WILDSIDE PRESS

Originally published in 1900. First book publication: 1905.
Published by Wildside Press LLC.
Visit us online at wildsidepress.com.

PREFACE

This story of the *Rival Ocean Divers* has been written especially for such boys as like tales of the deep blue sea.

A search for a hidden treasure is certain to be a fascinating one, and when the treasure is located at the bottom of the great ocean the quest is bound to become more or less perilous.

In opening this tale I had a twofold object in view. The first was to write a story which would interest boys, and the second was to unfold to their view a few of the marvels of deep-sea life, telling of the strange fish and other creatures to be found at the bottom of the Pacific Ocean.

In 1898 the United States government sent out an expedition to certain portions of the Pacific to test a new diving bell and a new machine for deep-sea soundings, and also to bring back such specimens of deep-sea animal and vegetable life as the expedition might be fortunate enough to obtain. The official report of this expedition is extremely interesting and useful, and from it the author has obtained much data of value, for use in the present work.

This story was originally used as a serial in a popular weekly. It seemed to please its readers, and the author hopes that in its present enlarged and rewritten form it will meet with equal favor.

Roy Rockwood.
April 1, 1905.

CHAPTER 1

PUNISHING A SNEAK

"A million at the bottom of the sea, father?"

"That is what I said, Dave."

"It is a fortune!"

"There may be more than that. But I am sure of the million."

"And it would belong to us if we found it?"

"Yes, every cent of it."

"But you say the Hankers lay claim to the fortune," went on Dave Fearless, a handsome lad of seventeen, the only son of Amos Fearless, ex-sea captain and marine architect.

"Yes, Lemuel Hankers always did claim the Washington fortune. His mother, you know, was a Washington."

"But so was your father."

"Exactly; and the money was left to our branch of the family, no matter what the Hankers may say to the contrary."

"And it was shipped from China to San Francisco in the steamship *Happy Hour*."

"Yes, but the *Happy Hour* belied her name, for she went down in the middle of the Pacific with all on board."

"And the exact location of this wreck?"

"Was not known up to six months ago. Then the *Albatross*, making some deep-sea fishing for the government, came upon some wreckage which proved conclusively that the *Happy Hour* had gone down in the exact spot which I have marked on the chart here."

"Do the Hankers know of this locality?"

"I think not. They were in Europe on a pleasure tour when the report came in, and it is very likely that it escaped their notice."

"You must be right, for they are very rich, and if they thought they could add to their fortunes they would fit out an expedition at once and go in search of the sunken treasure."

"Right you are, Dave. But they would have their hands full finding it, for you must remember, the Pacific Ocean at this point is nearly two miles deep."

"Two miles!" Dave Fearless' face fell. "Then we'll never see a single piece of that gold."

"I have been thinking of the matter for several weeks, and I think I have solved the problem of how to get to the wreck, if I can work the plan I have in mind," replied Mr. Fearless, as he began to pace the floor of the modest dining room thoughtfully.

"And what is your plan, father?"

"It is this: Two weeks from today our government is going to send another ship to the Pacific, the *Swallow*, under the command of Captain Paul Broadbeam."

"What, dear old Captain Broadbeam, whom we used to know at Nantucket Light?"

"The same, Dave. He will be in full charge of the expedition, which is to sound the depths of the Pacific, locate any new islands which may be brought to light, and drag the bottom of the ocean for strange fish or marine animals, for the Fish Commission. For this purpose the expedition will take along one of the new Costell diving bells."

"You mean one of those glass cages which they can lower to the bottom of the ocean and then walk around on big steel legs, like an artificial crab?"

"Exactly. They say they work perfectly, and if that is so, we ought to be able to get to the wreck of the *Happy Hour* and explore it without difficulty."

"We? Shall we go along with Captain Broadbeam?"

"If my application as master diver is accepted," and Amos Fearless smiled faintly.

"Then you've applied for such a position?"

"Yes. I did it as soon as I heard Broadbeam was in charge. I know he will do what he can for me."

"And what of me, father?"

"If I go, you shall go as assistant."

"Hurrah! Then the sunken treasure is as good as ours!"

"Don't be too sure, Dave. Even if we are successful, there is plenty of work cut out for us before we lay our hands on that million dollars, or any part of it. We must—what's that?"

Mr. Amos Fearless broke off short and ran to the window of the cottage in which he and his son lived. "A fellow running down to the beach! He was at the window listening!"

"It's Bart Hankers!" burst from Dave's lips. "Bart Hankers, of all people! He must have heard all we said."

"That's too bad!" Amos Fearless gave a deep sigh. "I wanted to keep this a secret."

"The miserable sneak!" went on Dave, indignantly. "I'm going after him and see what he means by such conduct."

And before his father could stop him, the lad was out of the cottage and running toward the beach at his best speed.

As said before, Dave Fearless was a youth of seventeen, tall, well-built, and handsome. He had been brought up along the coast of Long Island Sound, and had spent two years of his life in a lighthouse not far distant from his present residence in the village of Quanatack.

Following in the footsteps of his father, Dave had taken to the water naturally, and no boy on Long Island could swim better, row better, or handle a sailboat more skillfully than he. In addition to this, Dave had often been with his father when the latter was working at his trade as a master diver, and he knew more about the work of a diver than did many men who followed it for a living.

Father and son lived together by themselves, Mrs. Fearless having died several years before. Mr. Fearless had once been fairly well-to-do, but a fire, and the wild speculations of a brother, now dead also, had robbed him of all of his savings and left him with nothing but his hands to depend upon for a living.

The village in which the Fearlesses lived was not a large one, but it contained some people who were very friendly to the master diver and his son, and also contained some who were just the opposite.

Among the latter were Lemuel Hankers and his eighteen-year-old son Bart. The Hankers were distantly related to the Fearlesses, but as the latter were poor, the relationship was never acknowledged by the former. Indeed, Bart Hankers took particular pains to snub Dave Fearless upon every possible occasion.

Some of the snubbings flashed over Dave's mind as he sped after Bart Hankers, who was running to where he had left a small boat tied up at one of the village docks.

"I'll show him that he is not to play the sneak on us, even if he does snub me," muttered Dave, as he reached the dock, to find Bart just entering the rowboat.

In a minute he was at the stringpiece of the dock.

"Hi, Bart Hankers, I want to talk to you!" he called out.

"What do you want of me, Dave Fearless?" returned the rich youth, sullenly.

"I want to know what you mean by playing sneak around our house."

"Around your house? I haven't been near your house."

"Yes, you have. You just came from there."

"It's untrue. I have been up to Radley's store all the morning."

"I saw you and so did my father. You're a nice sneak, you are, I must declare. If I were you I'd be ashamed of myself."

"See here, if you call me a sneak, I'll punch your head for you, Dave Fearless!" howled Bart, angrily.

"Well, you are a sneak, so there!"

"So you want your head punched, do you?"

"If I do, you're not able to do the job."

"Won't I? I'll show you." And Bart leaped from the rowboat back to the dock.

"You were up under our window listening to the talk between my father and me."

"It isn't so!"

"It's the truth."

"You say another word and I'll thrash you within an inch of your life!" howled Bart, working himself up into a magnificent rage.

"I am not afraid of you," answered Dave, calmly. The fact that Bart was two inches taller than himself and weighed at least fifteen pounds more did not daunt him.

"Will you take back what you said?"

"Instead of taking it back, I repeat what I said—you are a mean sneak, and I want everybody in this village to know it," answered Dave, in a loud voice.

Several boys and a man were fishing near at hand, and now they drew closer to learn what was the cause of the trouble.

The man, who did some work for Mr. Hankers, sided with Bart, but the boys all favored Dave.

"Pitch into him, Dave," piped in one of the smaller lads. "He puts on too many airs, he does!"

"Don't you dare to touch Mr. Hankers," put in the man.

"I will do as I see fit, Hank Shores," retorted Dave. "Don't you interfere here."

"Never mind him, Shores," said Bart, with a sneer. "I can handle him well enough alone, and I'll give him all he wants, too."

"A fight! A fight!" exclaimed several of the boys, and soon a fair-sized crowd collected on the dock, for, in a village, a fight is a great event, to be talked over for many a day afterward.

"What's the trouble?" asked several.

"Dave Fearless and Bart Hankers are going to have it out."

"What started it?"

"Dave says Bart is nothing but a miserable sneak."

"You have got to take back what you said," blustered Bart, squaring off.

"I'll take back nothing," retorted Dave.

He had scarcely spoken when the rich youth struck out and landed lightly on his shoulder.

As quick as lightning Dave returned the blow, landing on Bart's nose with just sufficient force to draw blood.

"Ouow!" howled the rich youth, and staggered back.

"First blood for Dave Fearless!"

"Give him another like that, Dave!"

In a worse rage than ever Bart rushed at Dave again and this time caught him on the chin, and nearly knocked him down.

"There's one for Bart Hankers!"

"He'll down Dave Fearless yet!"

As quickly as he could Dave recovered and rushed at his opponent.

Blows now flew thick and fast, and Dave was hit on the shoulder, on the chest, and on the cheek.

But he returned every blow with interest, and Bart received a crack in the eye which made him see a thousand stars, and then another in the mouth, which loosened two of his teeth.

"Oh!" he groaned, and staggered toward the end of the dock.

"Have you had enough?" demanded Dave.

"No."

Hardly had Bart answered when Dave squared off again. Bart struck out feebly and Dave warded off the blow with ease.

Then Dave's left fist shot out, fairly and squarely, and the rich youth received a blow under the chin which lifted him off his feet and sent him backward with a loud splash into the waters of Long Island Sound.

CHAPTER 2

THE HANKERS' MOVE

"Bart's overboard!"

"My! But wasn't that a clever blow!"

"Dave is too many for him, even if Bart is larger."

So the cries ran on as all rushed to the edge of the dock.

Bart Hankers had disappeared, but he soon came up, spluttering and floundering around in a fashion to make many of those present laugh.

The water at the dock was not extra deep, and his head had become covered with black mud from the bottom.

"You—you—rascal!" he cried, when he could speak. "I'll—I'll have you locked up for that!"

"Locked up!" cried several. "What for? It was a fair fight."

"Dave had no right to knock him into the water," put in Hank Shores.

Bart Hankers' rowboat was close at hand and into this the rich boy climbed slowly and painfully, for he was still partly dazed by the crack under the chin.

His wet and muddy appearance made many in the crowd laugh.

"I say, Bart, you look as if you were dressed for the ball!" cried one boy.

"Now's the time to call on your best girl, Bart. You're in good shape for hugging her," added another.

"You fellows shut up!" growled the rich youth, shaking his fist at them. "If you don't I'll make it hot for the lot of you."

"About as hot as you made it for Dave Fearless, eh?" was the reply, and a shout of derision went up.

Then one of the boys began to throw some fish bait at Bart, and in a minute half a dozen youths were at it and Bart was struck in several places.

"Oh, I must get away from here," he muttered and then cried to Hank Shores: "Row me over to Purry's dock, will you, Shores?"

"I will," replied Shores, and leaping into the rowboat, took up the oars. Soon the craft was out of reach of those left behind. But before Bart got out of hearing he heard the village lads give a hurrah for Dave Fearless.

"All right, Dave Fearless," he muttered, under his breath. "You're on top this time, but I reckon my father and I will win in the long run."

"He played you foul, Bart," said Shores, soothingly. He was little better than a sneak himself.

"He wouldn't have been able to do it only I—er—I sprained my arm at rowing yesterday. That's why I got you to row for me," answered Bart. But what he said about his arm was a falsehood.

Half an hour later Bart Hankers entered his elegant home at the end of the main street of the village and sneaked up to the bathroom, where he washed up and changed his wet clothing for a dry suit. Then he went downstairs and to the library, where his father sat, reading the stock reports in a New York paper.

"Father, the mystery is solved," he said, as he closed the door carefully, that nobody might hear what he had to say but his parent.

Lemuel Hankers, a thin, yellow-skinned man of fifty, looked at his son curiously.

"What mystery, Bart?" he asked.

"The mystery of the missing Washington fortune."

"You don't mean it!" And the man leaped from his chair in astonishment.

"I do mean it."

"What have you learned?"

"I know where the *Happy Hour* went down."

"Where did you get your information?"

"From the Fearlesses."

"Do they know?"

"They do. Quite by accident I overheard Dave and his father talking."

"Indeed! Tell me the particulars," went on Lemuel Hankers.

Without a blush Bart related all he had overheard while eavesdropping at the window of the Fearless cottage. Hankers senior listened with close attention.

"It is a shame that we should have missed this information when it came in," he muttered. "We might already be on the way to recover the fortune."

"We ought to try and get that chart," said Bart.

"We won't want the chart. I can get the same news from the government that Amos Fearless has got."

"Let us go in search of the sunken treasure, dad. It certainly belongs to us."

"Of course it does, Bart. Yes, if this news is true, I will go after the missing million."

"But you will have to take expert divers along, and all that sort of thing."

"I can do that easily. I own stock in the San Francisco Wrecking Company, and it will not be difficult for me to charter one of their vessels, along with all the latest appliances for raising valuables from the ocean's depths."

"Then wouldn't it be advisable for us to start at once?"

"I must find out the particulars of this matter first."

"How will you do that?"

"The easiest way will be to make a trip to Washington."

"Then you had better go tonight."

"I will," answered Lemuel Hankers.

He was as good as his word, and the next day found him at Washington.

He quickly introduced himself to the proper parties and from them learned as much as Amos Fearless knew concerning the location of the wrecked *Happy Hour*. That the ship had been exactly located there could be no doubt. But it was also true that the ocean currents were gradually shifting the wreck from one position to another.

"If anything is to be done it must be done soon," he said, upon returning home. "That section of the ocean's bed is subject to earthquakes, and an earthquake might sink the *Happy Hour* so that no diver could find her again."

"Then why don't you start for San Francisco at once?"

"I will make up my mind inside of the next twenty-four hours," answered Lemuel Hankers.

"Of course, if you go you'll take me along," went on Bart.

"I wasn't thinking of doing so."

"I don't want to stay behind. Dave Fearless is going with his dad."

"But they are both expert divers and will do their own work, while I will have to have our work hired out."

"I don't care. I want to be on hand to see the Fearlesses outwitted."

"Very well then, you shall go," answered Lemuel Hankers.

The next day saw the rich man and his son on their way to San Francisco, to fit out an expedition to hunt for the sunken treasure.

CHAPTER 3

A STRANGE HOTEL ADVENTURE

"Father, I have news for you!" cried Dave Fearless, as he rushed into the cottage all out of breath.

"What now, Dave?"

"The Hankers have left Quanatack and gone to San Francisco."

"Impossible!"

"It's true. They took the train for New York, and Sam Dilks overheard Bart ask his father what the tickets to San Francisco would cost."

"That looks bad."

"And that isn't the worst of it. Sam also overheard them talking about the San Francisco Wrecking Company and heard Mr. Hankers say he felt sure he could get the vessel without delay."

"Then they must be after the sunken treasure beyond a doubt, Dave." Amos Fearless gave a slight groan. "They'll get the start of us after all!"

"How about that job for us on the *Swallow*?"

"I have heard nothing new."

"If I were you I'd send a long letter to Captain Broadbeam and let him know just how we stand."

"I will do it."

The letter was sent that night, and then the Fearlesses waited anxiously for a reply.

Two days later came a telegram from Washington. It was from their old friend the captain and ran as follows:

"Both engaged at salary mentioned in letter. Report here without delay."

"Hurrah! We're in it after all!" shouted Dave, flinging up his cap, and he danced a jig for joy. "Now for the Pacific Ocean and the missing fortune!"

Father and son had prepared everything for a start from home, and that evening saw them on the way to Washington. They spent the night in New York, and reported at the Capital City at noon the next day.

"Glad to see you," said Captain Broadbeam, shaking both by the hand. "Come over to my hotel and we'll talk matters over." He was a round-faced, jolly old sea-dog, and nobody could help liking him.

At the hotel the captain was let into the secret of the sunken treasure, in which he immediately took a deep interest. When Lemuel Hankers was mentioned he scowled.

"He is my enemy," he said. "He tried to get me out of my position so that some captain friend of his could have the berth. I'd be glad to knock the wind out o' his sails, consarn him!"

"Where is the *Swallow* now?"

"At San Francisco, all ready to sail."

"And when shall we go West?"

"Day after tomorrow, and you can go along with me."

A long talk followed, during which Amos Fearless asked about a diving bell.

"Yes, we have the very latest pattern on board of the *Swallow*," answered Captain Broadbeam, "and we shall also take along the very best of diving outfits, deep-sea sounders, and drag-nets—better even than those on the *Albatross*."

"Then we'll be fixed to go right ahead," said Mr. Fearless. "But we must get ahead of Lemuel Hankers and his son."

"Trust me to do that, Fearless. But when it comes to going down to a wreck as lies two miles under the surface o' the ocean, why, you and Dave will have to do that part o' the job."

"And we will," put in Dave, quickly. "I know it is a gigantic undertaking, but with the proper outfits, I feel convinced that we will get there sure!" and he shook his head confidently.

In secret Amos Fearless promised Captain Broadbeam twenty-five percent of any sum recovered from the wreck, providing the government would allow the officer to accept the amount.

It was not until late that night that the party separated and Dave and his father retired to a room in another part of the hotel.

When they left Captain Broadbeam, a man in a room next to the captain's got up from his knees, for he had been down listening at the keyhole of a door which connected the two apartments.

This fellow was named Pete Rackley, and he was in Lemuel Hankers' employ.

"I'm onto their game right enough," muttered Rackley to himself. "So they are going to outwit my boss? Well, I reckon not."

Before going to bed that night, Pete Rackley wrote a long letter to Lemuel Hankers, telling the rich man of what he had heard.

He felt that he must keep Dave and his father from going West to join the *Swallow*, no matter what the cost.

So he at once laid a plan to have Dave arrested for supposed pocket-picking.

The next morning he met Dave in the reading room, where he had gone to glance over the newspapers.

Unknown to Dave he approached the lad and dropped into his coat pocket a pocket-book containing ten dollars and a visiting card upon which was written his name, Peter Rackley.

Then he walked out into the hallway to the door of the hotel, stopped suddenly, and gave a cry:

"My pocket-book! It is gone!"

"What's that, sir?" demanded the hotel clerk, who happened to be passing.

"My pocket-book is gone! It must have been stolen from me!"

"Did it have much in it?"

"Ten dollars or more."

"Perhaps you dropped it, sir."

"Hardly. I had it quarter of an hour ago, when I was in the reading room. Ha, I have it! That young man took it from me." And Pete Rackley started back to the reading room.

"What young man?"

"The fellow who brushed up so close to me at the table. There he is!" Rackley ran up to Dave and caught him by the shoulder. "You thief!" he said. "Give me back my money!"

Of course Dave was taken completely by surprise.

"Your money?" he repeated. "I know nothing of your money."

"You must have it. Sir, will you have him searched?" went on Pete Rackley to the clerk.

"Certainly, he can search me if he wishes," said Dave, promptly. "I am no thief."

A few more words followed, and the clerk began to search Dave. Soon the pocket-book was brought to light, much to Dave's astonishment and dismay.

"Ha! What did I tell you!" said Pete Rackley. "Call an officer at once. I want this young rascal arrested on the spot!" and he caught hold of Dave again, that the youth might not escape.

CHAPTER 4

AN OCEAN MONSTER

Dave knew not what to say. Here he was accused of a robbery of which he knew absolutely nothing. The very prison doors seemed opening to receive him.

But while he stood there, not knowing what would happen next, an unexpected friend stepped up in the shape of a stranger, who had been reading in a corner.

"Excuse me, but there is something wrong here," said the stranger. "That man is no thief, to my way of thinking."

"What do you know of this?" demanded the hotel clerk.

"A short while ago I saw that man come up behind this young man and slip that pocket-book into his pocket. I thought at the time he was playing some friendly joke, but it seems he was up to something more serious."

At these words Pete Rackley turned deadly pale. He was caught in his own trap, and he knew it.

"It's false!" he began. "I—I—"

"I saw the action, too," put in another stranger. "I thought it very odd."

"We'll have the police investigate this," said the hotel clerk, and told a hallman to call an officer of the law.

This did not suit Pete Rackley at all.

"I—I guess there is some mistake," he stammered, and turning, he ran from the room and from the hotel. Although he had left a trunk behind him, he never came back to claim the property.

"That was a strange thing to do," said one of the strangers to Dave, after the excitement was over. "Is he your enemy?"

"He must be, but he is a stranger to me," answered our hero.

The trip to San Francisco was made without anything special happening, and soon Dave and his father found themselves on board of the *Swallow*, which lay at her dock taking on the last of her stores for the long trip around the Pacific Ocean.

After a number of inquiries, Amos Fearless learned that Lemuel Hankers had chartered the small steamer *Raven*, from the Wrecking Company, and had set sail on his treasure quest the day previous.

"Never mind, we'll make up for lost time when once we get started," said Captain Broadbeam. "I fancy the *Swallow* is a better boat in every way than the *Raven*."

Two days later the *Swallow* sailed with Mr. Fearless and Dave on board as master diver and assistant.

The diving outfits on board pleased the master diver very much, and he was likewise greatly interested in the diving bell the ship carried.

"That ought to be just the thing for our work," he said to Dave, "if they can let it down to where the wreck of the *Happy Hour* rests."

"But two miles is a tremendous distance, father."

"I know it. I have never yet gone down over three hundred feet."

"Perhaps we shall fail."

"We must try a short distance first, Dave. We can't go down those two miles at the start. Captain Broadbeam wishes us to go down tomorrow anyway, to hunt for some strange fish, said to be in these waters, a fish known by the scientific name of Eurypharynx Pelecanoides."

"What a fearful name!" muttered Dave. "Is the fish as bad?"

"Yes, and worse. The monster is said to be all of twenty feet long, with a head larger than a hogshead and a mouth seven feet across. Its body and tail are covered with spines or stickers, and its teeth are like so many large needles."

"Truly an ugly customer to meet," and Dave shuddered.

"I am afraid he'll be an ugly customer to bag—in a net or otherwise."

"Are we to use the diving bell?"

"Yes, we are to try it, but we are likewise to use our diving suits, too—just to try both outfits," returned the master diver.

The next day the *Swallow* reached a section of the Pacific where the strange fish described by Amos Fearless was supposed to exist, upon the bottom of the ocean bed, half a mile below the surface.

Diving suits were brought forth, and Mr. Fearless and Dave were not long in preparing to descend.

Then the diving bell was adjusted to a long wire rope and let over the side, and they entered this.

The word was given, and slowly but surely they descended into the cold and dark depths of the mighty Pacific.

At a distance of two hundred feet the bright sunshine overhead began to fade away, and at five hundred feet it was as black as night, that is, some distance away from the diving bell. But around the bell several electric lights in the apparatus made all as bright as day.

Down and down they went, the pressure on the diving bell becoming each second more powerful.

At such a depth no human being could have lived without something to protect him from a weight which was ever ready to crush anything from the outside world.

At last the diving bell rested on the bottom of the ocean, and Amos Fearless sent up the signal to stop lowering.

Then father and son inspected the ocean's bottom with much curiosity.

Here were numerous fish of curious shapes, but none of large size. There were also sea crabs, with sharp claws and protruding reddish eyes.

But no sign of the Eurypharynx Pelecanoides, the wonderful fish of which they had been sent in search.

"It seems to be safe enough," said Dave to his father, in the sign language of divers. "Let us go outside and look around."

"But not too far away from the diving bell," answered the master diver. "The pressure may make us sick, and then we'll have to get inside again as quickly as possible."

Soon they were ready, and with a fresh supply of air in their helmets, they stepped out upon the slimy, black surface of the ocean's bottom.

At sight of them the small fish thrashed around wildly, and the sea crabs scampered in all directions.

With caution they moved away from the bell to where the bottom appeared to slope downward.

Here there was a large hole, and they wondered what might be at its bottom.

Dave was well in advance, when of a sudden a strange sensation brought him to a halt and made him glance to his left.

A shriek of terror burst from his lips.

The dreadful Eurypharynx Pelecanoides had appeared, and was making swiftly towards him. The terrific mouth of the monster was wide open, as if to swallow him alive!

CHAPTER 5

FROM ONE DANGER INTO ANOTHER

"I am lost!"

Such was the agonizing thought which crossed Dave Fearless' mind when he beheld himself confronted by the fish known as the Eurypharynx Pelecanoides, commonly called the Sea Devil of the Ocean's Bottom.

The monster was all of twenty feet long, with a head closely resembling a black rubber balloon. Its eyes shone like two electric-light globes, while its mouth opened and shut with a strange, clicking sensation which went through the young diver like the piercing of a needle.

Dave's thought was to retreat to the diving bell, but this seemed impossible, for the monstrous fish was only a few yards off and approaching rapidly. It looked as if in another moment all would be over and he would be swallowed alive, like Jonah of old.

A million thoughts rushed through his brain—thoughts of his younger days, of his happy life around the lighthouse—and of how the Hankers might yet triumph over his father and himself. In the meanwhile the monster came closer, and now it emitted from its mouth a horrible green slime, with which to cover its victim before swallowing him, after the manner of its cousin on earth, the boa constrictor.

But at this moment, when the youth seemed surely lost, something happened as quickly as it was unexpected, and which changed the whole course of events.

Through the black waters rushed another fish, long, thin, and exceedingly bony. From the snout of this fish stuck a sword-like spear, fully three feet long, with a point like that of a dart.

This was the Devil's Needle, another monster of the deep, and dreaded by all other monsters, for it is the deadly enemy of everything that crosses its path.

There was a strange, hissing sound, a thrust, and the sword-like spear was thrust into the side of the Eurypharynx Pelecanoides.

It was like sticking into an inflated bladder.

The water was at once dyed crimson and the mighty ocean monster swept back and then began to thrash around wildly, sending mud and sand, slime and blood, flying in all directions.

As quickly as it had appeared, the Devil's Needle now disappeared.

Too faint to stand, Dave sank back on the ocean bottom.

But his father was close at hand, and with rare presence of mind he caught up his son and carried him to the diving bell.

In another moment both were inside of the machine and had the door bolted.

They were now, as they thought, safe from harm, and Amos Fearless lost no time in turning the electric light of the diving bell upon the Sea Devil of the Ocean's Bottom.

It was still thrashing around in a circle, but gradually its struggles became fainter, and at last it lay quiet.

"He's done for," said the parent, in the divers' sign language. "I will fasten him to the bottom of the bell and then signal them on the ship to haul up."

"Be careful," cautioned Dave. "That other fish may serve you as he just served that horrible creature."

"We will move the diving bell close to the dead creature," answered Amos Fearless.

This was done without much difficulty, by means of a set of levers which connected with the artificial steel claws of the diving bell.

Then Amos Fearless went forth once more, taking with him a short chain, which he began to fasten around the slimy and sticky body of the dead Sea Devil.

The job was a nasty one, but this could not be helped, and therefore he made the best of it.

He had just finished the work when Dave saw the Devil's Needle again approaching.

So far the fish had not seen Mr. Fearless, but now it spotted him and made a dart forward as if to thrust the old diver through and through with that bony sword.

Dave's heart leaped into his throat, for he imagined nothing could save his father from death.

But then came the thought of moving the diving bell into the fish's path.

He grabbed two of the levers and pushed them down, violently.

Acting under the impetus thus given, the diving bell made a stride forward, directly in the path of the Devil's Needle.

Crash!

Full against the steel frame of the bell came the sword-like spear of the fish.

Another crack followed, as the spear was broken off close to the creature's snout.

The great shock stunned the Devil's Needle and it turned over on its side and sank slowly to the ocean's bottom.

Realizing that something was wrong, Amos Fearless turned, just in time to witness the breaking off of the bony spear.

He started for the diving bell, then of a sudden changed his plan of action.

One of the diving bell's steel claws lay close to the Devil's Needle, and this he raised up and placed over the monster.

Dave, inside of the bell, understood, made the lever work, and immediately the claw fastened itself around the body of the half-stunned fish.

Then Amos Fearless picked up the broken-off sword spear and re-entered the bell.

In a moment more the signal was given to rise, and slowly the diving bell went up to the surface of the ocean, dragging the bodies of the two deep-sea monsters with it.

"A glorious find!" cried Captain Broadbeam, when the two monsters were hoisted on board of the *Swallow*.

"Yes, but we don't want to make another such find under the same circumstances," answered Amos Fearless. And then he related the particulars of the adventure on the bottom of the ocean.

There were two scientists on board of the ship and they went to work at once to prepare the bodies of the two fish which had been caught.

"That sword spear can be fastened on again," said one of the learned gentlemen. "And then the specimen will be practically perfect."

"Folks at home ought to see them alive," said Dave. "I never saw such a horrible sight in my life!"

"These fish could not live in ordinary water," was the answer. "See, the breathing apparatus on each is already bursting. They can only live at a depth of half a mile or more. If one tried to reach the surface by swimming upward, it would only be committing suicide."

"I don't quite understand the reason for that, sir."

"It is simple, my lad. You know the air around us presses us on every inch of our bodies, and we are built to resist that pressure. An ordinary fish is built to resist the pressure of ordinary water. Such a fish as the Sea Devil is built to resist the pressure of hundreds of pounds to the square inch, and consequently when it is brought up, the pressure inside is too great for the pressure outside, and that destroys the breathing power of the marine animal," concluded the learned man.

By evening the *Swallow* was on her way westward once more and the scientific men had the specimens almost ready to be placed in huge tanks of alcohol.

So far, nothing had been seen or heard of the *Raven*, but a strict watch was kept each day for the Hankers' vessel.

But one more stop was to be made, at the island of San Murio, and then the *Swallow* was to proceed directly for the locality where the treasure ship *Happy Hour* had gone down.

Day after day passed and nothing of importance occurred.

One afternoon there was some slight break in the machinery and the ship had to come to a stop for a couple of hours while repairs were being made.

It was a hot day and several of the sailors readily obtained permission to go in swimming.

"I think I will join them," said Dave to his father. "The water looks cool and tempting."

"All right, Dave," was the answer. "But take care you don't get a cramp."

"If I do, you can bet I'll yell for help," laughed the young diver.

He was soon in the water and sporting around to his heart's content.

The sailors had allowed one of the small boats to drift astern, and Dave swam to this and showed several of them how to make deep dives and long stretches under the ocean's surface.

The party were in the midst of having a lot of fun when a thrilling cry came from the ship.

"A shark! A shark! Beware of the shark!"

All gazed in the direction pointed out, and saw a huge shark approaching rapidly, as if prepared to devour one or another of them!

CHAPTER 6

STRUCK BY LIGHTNING

"We will be devoured!"

"Swim for the ship, boys!"

"See, he is coming this way!"

"Save me, somebody! Save me!"

Such were some of the cries which rang out as the sailors swam, terror-stricken, in one direction or another.

In the meantime the shark came on rapidly. He was a big creature, with a cruel-looking mouth and teeth that were equally ugly.

At first he turned toward one of the sailors, who was swimming for the ship.

But a rope was thrown to the tar, and this he grasped and was hauled on board with all rapidity.

Then the shark turned for another of the sailors.

But this fellow was making for the small boat, and soon he was on board and safe for the time being.

Then the shark turned swiftly and came for Dave.

The youth dove at once, remembering that a shark can attack under water only with difficulty.

But the boy could not remain under the surface forever, and at last he had to come up, this time somewhat closer to the *Swallow*.

But the shark saw him and turned again to attack the young diver.

It was a critical moment, and Dave was about to give himself up for lost when a shot rang out, followed by another.

Amos Fearless had been in the cabin when the shout of "Shark!" was raised.

Knowing at once the peril of the situation, he had caught a gun from the cabin wall and lost no time in hurrying to the deck.

The shark was still ten feet away from Dave when Mr. Fearless fired.

The first bullet struck the monster in the side, doing little damage.

But the shark turned his head to learn what had hit him and in a twinkle Amos Fearless discharged the weapon a second time.

This time the bullet struck the shark squarely in the eye and entered the marine creature's brain.

Up leaped the shark, clear above the water, to fall with a shock that sounded like the report of a cannon.

The water flew in all directions, drenching all who stood at the rail of the *Swallow* taking in the appalling situation.

In its death agonies the shark hurled itself against the ship, lifting its tail clear to the rail and wrecking a portion of the woodwork.

Then it turned and dove for the small boat.

The sailor on board had just time enough to leap out and dive, when the marine creature struck it with all force, smashing the rowboat to atoms.

But that was the last act of the shark. In a minute more it was dead, and floated on the bosom of the ocean close to the ship.

A line was thrown to Dave and the sailors, and all were hauled on board.

"My boy! My boy!" murmured Amos Fearless. "What a narrow escape for you!"

"You saved my life, father!" replied Dave. He could scarcely speak, but the grip he gave his parent's hand meant a good deal.

Some of the sailors wanted to bring the shark's remains on board, to get the teeth, and Captain Broadbeam consented, and later on, the scientists on the *Swallow* prepared the skeleton for mounting, to be sent to the Smithsonian Institution at Washington.

It remained very warm, and Captain Broadbeam looked constantly for a storm.

"Almost all ships catch 'em in these latitudes," he remarked to Dave. "This may be a long time a-coming, but it will pay up for lost time when it does come."

In this surmise Captain Broadbeam was correct.

Two days later, while the sun was shining brightly, there appeared a cloud to the southwest, scarcely bigger than a man's hand.

But the cloud grew larger with great rapidity, until it covered half the sky, and the sunlight was shut out and soon all became as dark, almost, as night. The wind began to blow and soon the waves were running higher and higher.

"We must run into the teeth of the storm," said the captain, and gave orders to change the course.

Presently it began to rain, and then followed lightning and thunder which were almost incessant.

"Never saw anything to match it," declared Dave, as he put on his oilskins and joined his father on the stern deck. "This beats those we had off Long Island all to pieces!"

"Right you are, Dave," answered Amos Fearless. "Take good care that you are not swept overboard."

The storm increased in violence until the *Swallow* was heaving and pitching as never before. At one moment she would be riding on the top of a very mountain of water, at the next she would be going down and down into a tremendous hollow that looked as if it would swallow up the stanch ship forever.

Captain Broadbeam surveyed the storm with anxiety, for he realized that it was unusually severe, and threatened the very existence of his craft.

The lightning played all around the metalwork of the ship, and the roar of the thunder was deafening.

"You had better go below," said the captain to Dave and his father. "You can do nothing on deck."

"Yes, we will go below," answered Amos Fearless. "Come, my son," and he led the way down into the cabin.

All of the ports and doors had been closed, and the air was stifling in the shut-up apartment, but of this there was no use to complain.

All crockery, glassware, and other loose objects had long since been secured, or they would have been flung in every direction.

Dave sat down in a chair screwed to the floor, and did his best to keep his seat.

At one moment he felt like pitching forward, at the next he seemed about to turn a back somersault.

The electric light burned dimly, for the electricity in the air had affected the circuit.

"We can be thankful when we are out of this," observed Mr. Fearless, as he, too, clung to a chair. "I never dreamed it could blow so hard and keep it up. In our eastern storms there is generally a lull every few minutes."

"I wonder if the *Raven* is in this, father?"

"There is no telling. This storm-center may be but a few miles in diameter."

"I am almost tempted to wish the *Raven* at the bottom of the ocean."

"That wouldn't be right, Dave."

"I know. But supposing they get ahead of us and the Hankers scoop in the Washington fortune?"

"Then we will have to pocket our loss and make the best of it."

"But our claim is better than theirs."

"Morally, yes. But you must remember that legally the fortune will belong to whoever finds it, for it was abandoned at sea many years ago."

"I suppose that is so."

"For my part, Dave, I believe that neither of us will have an easy job to obtain the fortune. It is going to be a great task to even reach the sunken wreck."

"Oh, I know that. But the diving bell will help us."

"It will help a great deal. But you must remember the wreck may be turned over, or buried almost out of sight in the mud of the ocean bottom. In that case we'll have a lot of work to do before any of us can get into the ship and even locate the lost treasure."

"Never mind, father, the amount to be gained will be well worth all the trouble we will take to gain it."

"To be sure, for such a vast sum isn't picked up more than once in a life-time, even at the best. We can be certain—Heavens! What's that?"

Amos Fearless broke off short, and with good reason.

A fearful shock had come, as a bolt of lightning struck the forward works of the *Swallow*.

Then followed a strange hissing as the lightning played over the electric wires of the ship.

A blinding flash entered the cabin, followed by a crack as of a pistol, and Dave, half stunned, saw his father pitch forward across the table like one dead!

CHAPTER 7

"I CANNOT TALK!"

"Father! Tell me that you are alive! That you are not dead!"

Such was the agonizing cry which issued from Dave's lips as he gazed upon his parent.

Amos Fearless' face was like chalk, his eyes were set, and he certainly looked as if the breath of life had gone from him forever.

The *Swallow* was rolling and pitching so fearfully that for the time being the young man could do but little.

Yet he raised a cry which quickly brought the cabin boy to his side.

"What's up?" asked the boy, and then, seeing the stilled form, he continued: "Is he dead?"

"I—I hope not. But send Doctor Barrell here at once."

Doctor Barrell was one of the scientists attached to the expedition. He was a learned man, and Dave felt certain that if anything could be done for his parent, Doctor Barrell could do it.

The cabin boy went off with difficulty, and it was fully ten minutes before he returned with the medical man.

In the meantime, Dave laid his parent on the floor.

By placing his ear to his parent's breast, he found that his father still breathed faintly.

He was just pouring water over the sufferer's face when Doctor Barrell came in.

"What is the trouble?" he asked. "Has he had a tumble? I do not wonder; I have tumbled twice myself."

"No, he has been struck by lightning, doctor. Please do all you can for him."

"Struck by lightning! In here? How?"

"The lightning entered on the electric-light wire and he got the full force of the shock. I was partly stunned myself."

"I don't wonder. Yon can thank your stars that both of you are not dead."

"But my father?"

Before replying to this query, Doctor Barrell proceeded to make a thorough examination.

In the midst of this, Amos Fearless opened his eyes and stared around him, feebly.

But he could not move his tongue.

"He will live," said the doctor, slowly. "But—"

"But what, sir?"

"He may not be able to—that is, he has had a very heavy shock."

"Yes, yes! But what will he not be able to do?" questioned Dave, quickly.

"Perhaps I had better not answer that question just yet, David. There is no use of alarming you," and the physician turned away to prepare some medicines for the sufferer.

The night to follow was an anxious one to Dave.

Despite the storm, which did not let up for an instant, he remained constantly by his parent's side.

It was daybreak before Amos Fearless was pronounced out of danger.

He still lay in a semi-dazed condition, but his heart-beats were growing stronger every hour.

"In a few days he will probably be able to be around," said the doctor, and then he turned away to hide his troubled looks from Dave.

The youth saw the action and was more worried than ever.

As soon as the storm had abated and something could be cooked, he had a bowl of nourishment made for his father.

The sufferer swallowed a few spoonfuls, and that was all, and even that little went down with difficulty.

"Do you feel better, father?" he asked, soothingly.

Slowly Amos Fearless nodded. His lips moved slightly, but no intelligible sound came from them.

"Don't try to talk," went on the boy. "Take it easy and you will be yourself in a few days."

Again Mr. Fearless nodded, and then fell back, to doze off again.

The next day he was strong enough to sit up. The storm was now over and the *Swallow* was proceeding on her way to the island at which she was to stop.

"You are better now, surely," said Dave, speaking as cheerfully as he could.

For answer, Amos Fearless pointed to his mouth and then made a motion as if writing on paper.

A sudden horror seized Dave, causing a cold chill to run down his backbone.

"What is it?" he cried. "Oh, father, can't you speak?"

Again the old diver made a motion as if writing, and Dave hurriedly brought him a pencil and a writing pad.

Quickly Amos Fearless set down the following:

"My tongue is paralyzed and I cannot talk."

As Dave read the words, his very heart seemed to stop beating.

His father had become a mute!

The shock was an awful one.

He turned to the doctor, who had just come in.

"See what my father has written!" he cried. "Oh, doctor, cannot something be done?"

"It is what I feared," replied Doctor Barrell, gravely. "I have known of such cases before. I had such a case to treat in Richmond, about six years ago."

"And the sufferer—does he talk now?" was Dave's eager question.

Doctor Barrell shook his head, slowly.

"I am sorry to say he does not, although in every other respect he is a perfectly healthy man."

"But my father—cannot you give me some hope?"

"Let us hope for the best, David."

"You will do all you can for him?"

"To be sure I will."

The day was a perfect one, but Dave was utterly downcast and refused to be comforted.

The thought that his parent might remain a mute forever almost unnerved him.

"I'd rather lose the sunken treasure," he groaned to himself.

At nightfall the *Swallow* came in sight of the island of San Murio, and dropped anchor in a little bay surrounded by palms and other tropical trees.

The scene was a beautiful one, and had Dave's mind been free from care he would have enjoyed it thoroughly.

Amos Fearless was brought on deck and made comfortable in a steamer chair.

He was gaining strength rapidly, and the doctor expected the old diver to be around again in a week or ten days.

But he could not use his tongue for talking purposes, although he had little trouble in swallowing food.

Early the next morning some of the sailors from the *Swallow* were sent ashore for water.

"I wouldn't mind going," said Dave, in reply to a question from Captain Broadbeam. "But I hate to leave father."

Amos Fearless overheard this and at once wrote on a pad:

"Go, Dave, and have a good time. I'll be all right. This will be your last chance to stretch your legs on shore for many weeks to come."

So the young diver went ashore with the men, and while the sailors filled their water casks, Dave and a young engineer of the ship, named Bob Vilett, went off on a hunt, taking with them a shotgun and a rifle.

They had heard that numerous wild goats lived upon the island of San Murio, and thought to bag several of these by way of diversion.

"And who knows but what we'll bring down something larger, too!" said Bob Vilett, who was in his way quite a sportsman.

The *Swallow* was to remain at her anchorage until the next morning, so the pair had the whole day before them. Dave carried a pouch full of food, and Bob a good-sized water bottle, so that they were well provided, even if they did not bring down anything worth eating.

"Take good care of yourselves," said Captain Broadbeam, on parting with them. "Don't run into danger."

"We'll be careful," answered Dave, and off the pair set, never dreaming of the strange adventure and the grave peril in store for them.

CHAPTER 8

A DISASTROUS HUNT

The island of San Murio is not over six miles wide by twenty miles long. It is composed of two lines of hills, with a deep valley between. The hills are rocky and much broken, and there are numerous waterfalls and tiny brooks, as well as cliffs and caverns. The growth of trees and underwood is dense, and Dave and his friend had frequently all they could do to push their way along.

Both were in fine spirits, and Bob was inclined to burst into song, only Dave silenced him.

"If you sing you'll surely scare all the game away," he said. "A wild goat will hear your voice half a mile off."

"Right you are, Dave," returned Bob. "However, I can't repress my spirits when I'm ashore. It's so much better than being down in the hot and stuffy engine room of a steamship," and Bob threw down his rifle and made a handspring or two, after which he resumed his walk, feeling better.

A half-hour's journey brought them close to the top of the first series of hills, at a point opposite a small inland lake.

"Go slow now," whispered Bob. "There may be goats beyond."

They peered over the top of the hill with care, and sure enough, down at the lake shore they made out two large goats and two kids, all drinking.

"Take the one to the right, and I'll take the one to the left!" said Bob, in a low voice. "Ready? Then fire!"

Crack! Bang! went the rifle and the shotgun, and both of the large goats were seen to leap up and back as though struck.

But neither was fatally wounded, and both started to run slowly around the lake shore, to the line of hills on the opposite side, with the kids following.

"Come, we had better go after 'em!" said Bob, and led the way, and Dave followed, both reloading as they ran.

It was no easy task to reach the lake front, and by that time the goats were rushing up the hills opposite.

"Fire again!" cried Dave, and blazed away, bringing his game to its knees. Bob also fired, but missed his mark. Then on they went again, over rocks and stubble and through a mass of trailing vines, to where Dave's goat had gone down. The animal was dead.

"Good for you!" cried Bob. "Now I must do as well!" and away he went again, with Dave at his heels, anxious, if possible, to add the kids to his bag.

At the top of the second line of hills the wounded goat made a sharp turn to the left.

On went the young hunters after him, never dreaming of the pitfall into which they were rushing.

They were now side by side, and Bob was on the point of blazing away at the wounded goat, in full view before him, when Dave clutched his arm.

"Back!"

"What's up?"

"Nothing's up, but we'll be down if we don't take care!"

"What do you mean?"

Before Dave could reply, Bob saw what had caused the young diver to become alarmed.

They were walking over some moss and brushwood, and the mass under their feet was shaking like so much jelly.

Both started to retreat, but it was too late! Down went the mass of brushwood, at first slowly and then swifter and swifter.

They tried to clutch at the sides of the opening, but in vain. Everything they grasped gave way—sticks, moss, stones, bushes, vines. Nothing could stop that downward course.

The moss was dry and the dust filled their eyes, almost blinding them.

"We are lost!" gasped Bob, and then the dust got into his throat and he began to cough as though choking.

In the excitement of the moment, Dave's shotgun went off, the charge passing directly between him and his companion.

After falling about twenty feet, the mass of brushwood became wedged tight for a moment, and stopped descending.

"Oh!" came from Dave. "Now we are in a pickle. How are we to get out?"

For the moment they scarcely dared to move.

Then Bob took a step forward and the young diver did the same.

Instantly the mass began to sink once more, at first slowly and then as rapidly as ever.

Down they went—thirty feet, forty, fifty, sixty—a hundred, until the top of the hole was lost to sight and they found themselves they knew not where.

Again the brushwood and moss became wedged fast. But now they did not dare to move for fear of dislodging it once more.

"We are lost!" came from the engineer. "We'll never get out of this alive!"

"Don't give up yet," answered Dave, bravely, yet his heart felt like a lump of lead in his bosom.

"Where can we be?"

"Down in a mighty deep hole."

"I know. But is this the bottom?"

"There's no telling. We might—we are going down again!"

It was true. They were again descending, but now slowly, as if the passage below was growing smaller.

"Shall we ever stop!" groaned Dave.

"It's all up with us!" came from Bob. "We won't be able—gracious! Water!"

The young engineer was right.

The mass of brushwood had reached the level of some water at the bottom of the hole.

Down they sank, into this. First up to their ankles, then to their knees, then to their waists.

"We shall be drowned!" cried Dave.

"It looks like it," gasped Bob. "Heaven save us!"

Soon the water was up to their necks and still the stuff under them continued to sink.

Were they to be drowned like rats in a trap?

CHAPTER 9

A PRISONER UNDERGROUND

"What's to do now?"

The question came from Bob Vilett.

The sinking of the brushwood had ceased, and he and Dave found themselves in water almost up to their chins, in absolute darkness.

"I'm sure I don't know, Bob," was the young diver's response. "We are in a tight box, and no mistake."

"We can't stay here forever."

"True, but if we make a move we may sink deeper than ever, and then it will be all up with us."

A dead silence of several minutes followed. Presently both of the lads grew desperate.

"We'll have to do something, that's certain," Dave began, when of a sudden the driftwood sank once more, and they found themselves struggling wildly in the black waters at the bottom of the hole.

They were soon over their heads, and now found a strong current carrying them they knew not where. They had hold of each other, but soon the force of the water wrenched them apart.

Down and down went Dave, and turned over half a dozen times.

He felt as if he must be journeying toward the center of the earth, when he reached out his hand and struck a series of smooth rocks.

He tried to hold fast, but this was impossible, and in a twinkle he turned over again, and then his feet struck on something of a sandy beach.

Hardly knowing what he was doing, he stepped forward, and then found himself clear of the water.

This set him to running, and on he went until he brought up with much force against a stone wall, and fell back partly stunned.

His feet lay in the water, but his head was on the sand, and thus he remained for fully a quarter of an hour, unable to move.

There was a strange ringing in his ears, and when he at last arose his head ached as if it would split open.

"Oh!" he groaned, and staggered up the sand to the smooth, rocky wall.

Then he fell again, and did not move until half an hour later, when his head felt somewhat better.

Where was he, and how could he save himself?

These questions were easy to ask, but no answer was at hand, and he sank down much disheartened.

Then he suddenly roused himself and called loudly:

"Bob! Bob Vilett! Where are you?"

Again and again his voice was raised, but only a dismal echo answered him.

Was his late companion dead?

It was more than likely.

The tears sprang unbidden to the young diver's eyes, but he dashed them away.

He must save himself, no matter what the cost.

He realized that he had been saved from death by drowning only because he was used to being under water a long time without taking a breath.

All divers practice this art, for possible use should anything become the matter with their diving outfits while at work.

He felt in his clothing and found his water-proof matchbox still safe.

Soon he had a tiny light, and seeing some dry driftwood at hand he set it on fire.

The blaze threw grotesque shadows on the rocky walls around him, but revealed nothing to his gaze but those same walls and the silent, underground stream flowing between them.

He was entombed alive!

Gradually this conviction forced itself upon him, causing him to shiver as if with the ague.

Again he called out the name of his late companion, and again only the dull echoes answered him.

He reckoned that he must be at least a hundred yards from the hole made by the sunken driftwood.

To get back to the hole, therefore, was out of the question.

He thought the matter over for a while, and then, taking up some driftwood for a torch, walked slowly along the sandy shore of the black stream.

Presently he came to a bend, and here found that the stream shot downward, forming an underground waterfall.

"I can't go in that direction," he reasoned. "I want to go up, not down."

The stream was less than twelve feet wide, and did not run so swiftly but what he could cross it without much danger.

Obtaining a fresh firebrand, for the first was now burnt out, he swam over to the opposite shore and began an investigation on that side.

"Hurrah!"

The exclamation escaped from his lips involuntarily.

The firebrand had dropped from his hand into the stream, leaving him in darkness.

Looking at the rocks, he had beheld a thin shaft of light striking down from some opening above.

"An opening! May it prove a way of escape!"

With a prayer for aid on his lips, Dave began to climb the rocks as best he could until he reached a hollow ten feet above the stream.

Here the light was stronger, and by applying his eyes to a long, narrow slit in the rocks he made out a broad cave beyond, the further end of which was wide open to the sunlight.

But how was he to get into the cave?

The opening was not over six inches wide, too narrow for the passage of his body.

The rocks were large, weighing several hundreds of pounds apiece.

To move them would take tools, and he had nothing.

Again in a state bordering on despair, he sat down to review his situation.

At last he leaped up, and clenching his hands, cried loudly:

"I must get out! I simply must!"

The cry was an inspiration, for, getting on his knees, he felt around and found that two of the big rocks were unsteady upon their resting places.

He pulled away at the smaller stones beneath, and soon had them loosened.

He continued his labors, and presently, with a mighty crash, one of the rocks slid down into the stream, disappearing beneath the surface with a splash.

At once the light from beyond shot into the opening. He was free!

His heart gave a bound of joy, and quickly he scrambled through the hole and into the cave beyond.

This was a large affair, being at least forty feet wide and high, and several hundred feet long.

"Now, if only Bob were safe, all would be well," thought the young diver.

Without waiting to light another torch he began to move toward the outer opening of the cave.

But before he had gone half the distance he came to a halt with a cry of dismay.

The cave was crossed by another underground stream, all of twenty feet wide, and flowing onward with tremendous swiftness.

It came out from under one rocky wall and disappeared under the wall opposite.

Taking a bit of driftwood, Dave threw it into the water, and it flashed out of sight instantly.

"I can't swim across that," he thought, dismally. "To attempt it would be foolhardy."

Now what was to be done?

He examined the walls carefully.

They were perfectly smooth, thus affording hold for neither foot nor hand.

"If the stream weren't quite so wide I might jump it," he reasoned. "But I—somebody is coming!"

He was right; somebody was entering the cave from the outer end.

The newcomers were two men, one dressed in the suit of an American business man and the other in the garb of a sailor.

"We'll be alone here and can talk the matter over without fear of interruption," said one of the pair, the man in ordinary clothes.

His voice sounded strangely familiar, and Dave strained his eyes to catch a better sight of him and of his companion.

Then, astonished beyond measure, the young diver dropped out of sight behind a rock bordering the underground stream he had been trying to cross.

The newcomers were Lemuel Hankers, the man who had set sail in the *Raven* after the sunken treasure, and Pete Rackley, the rascal who in Washington had accused Dave of robbing him!

CHAPTER 10

DAVE OVERHEARS A PLOT

"They are here for no good purpose!"

Such was the thought which crossed Dave's mind immediately after making his astonishing discovery.

As much as he wished to be saved from his present direful situation, he resolved to keep his presence a secret.

These men were his enemies, and by instinct he felt that Pete Rackley must be Lemuel Hankers' tool.

"I'll wager old Hankers had him try that game on me in Washington," thought the young diver. "It was done so that I couldn't join the *Swallow* at San Francisco, and that father might remain behind, too, to get me out of the scrape."

Presently Lemuel Hankers and Pete Rackley came so close that Dave could hear all that was said with ease.

"It is a surprise to me that the *Swallow* stopped here," Lemuel Hankers was saying. "Do you think she was following us?"

"Can't say as to that," replied Rackley, puffing away at a short pipe he was carrying. "Anyway, she's here. Now what is your game? Out with it."

"The game is that I don't want the Fearlesses to get at the sunken treasure, Pete."

"I've heard that before, Lemuel."

"You have always been my right-hand man, Pete, and I know I can rely on you yet, even though you did make a fizzle of that affair in Washington."

"I didn't know I was being spotted," growled the sailor, for such Pete Rackley really was.

"My game is that you go aboard of the *Swallow* and ship with Captain Broadbeam. Tell him you are a castaway, and have been here nearly a year."

"But young Fearless knows me."

"You can dye your face and your hair and he won't recognize you, I am sure. In that sailor rig you don't look like the man you were in Washington in a light suit and a linen shirt."

"That's true, too. But after I am on the *Swallow* I don't see what I can do to keep them from going ahead to where the treasure is."

"I will tell you what to do. Wait until you are about a day out from here and then watch your chance and disable the machinery, so that they will have to put back for repairs. When the machinery is repaired, injure the rudder, and that will bring them back again. Keep that up for about a month, and the treasure will be mine, and if I get it, you shall have ten thousand dollars in cold cash for your work."

"It's taking a big risk," answered Pete Rackley, slowly.

"And so is ten thousand dollars a big sum of money, Pete. It's more than you'll ever get by working, and you know it."

"That's true, too."

"And if you are sly about it, you'll run very little risk of detection."

"But how will I get on board of the *Raven* again?"

"After you have kept the *Swallow* behind a month you can let her go and desert, hiding in the woods so that they can't find you. You can provide yourself with plenty of food. As soon as we have the treasure on board of the *Raven*, I'll come back for you and take you on board."

"You won't desert me?"

"I will not. More than that, I'll take Captain Nesik into the secret with me, and I'll leave behind all of my diamonds and my gold watch as an evidence of my good faith."

"Leave your boy Bart here for company and I'll take you up, Hankers."

"I would even do that, Pete, but you know well enough Bart won't stay behind. He is crazy to get the treasure and crow over the Fearlesses. He even says he is going down himself, in that new diving bell we brought along— just to show that he can work under water as well as Dave Fearless."

"Then you must leave me all the stuff you can, and you and Captain Nesik must promise on your bended knees to come back for me. I wouldn't be marooned for twice ten thousand dollars."

"It will be all right. You can—hullo, who is calling?"

A form had appeared at the mouth of the cave.

"Are you in there, dad?" came the cry.

"Yes, Bart," answered Lemuel Hankers. He turned to Pete Rackley. "Come, quick! Do you accept my offer?"

"I do," answered the rascally sailor, and the pair of villains shook hands.

"What are you up to?" went on Bart Hankers, as he came closer.

"Oh, we were just taking a look around," replied his father, carelessly.

"Do you know that the *Swallow* is in this port?" went on Bart, as he drew closer to the underground stream.

"Yes."

"I wish she was at the bottom of the Pacific, and the Fearlesses with her."

"You should not be so hard on them," replied Lemuel Hankers, hypo-critically.

At this Pete Rackley gave a harsh laugh.

"You're a good one," he remarked in a low tone.

"Hush; I don't want my son to know too much," whispered Lemuel Hankers.

By this time Bart Hankers was standing on the edge of the underground stream.

"Wish I could cross over and see what's on the other shore," he muttered.

So far Dave had kept silent, drinking in all that was said.

He realized only too well what a plot was going on against his father and himself, and against the *Swallow*.

"If only I can get free, I'll show them a trick or two," he told himself.

Suddenly Bart Hankers uttered a cry.

"A snake! A snake!"

He was right; a long snake had appeared at the top of the underground stream.

It was a dangerous-looking reptile, eight feet long, and with nasty green eyes.

Bart Hankers fell back in confusion.

But instead of climbing to the outer bank, the snake crawled out close to the rock behind which Dave was in hiding.

It was against human nature to remain hidden under the circumstances, and the young diver leaped up with all rapidity.

At the same time he yelled at the snake, and the reptile, much startled, dropped back into the stream and was lost to view.

"Dave Fearless!" gasped Bart Hankers, as soon as the danger from the snake was past.

"That boy!" came from Lemuel Hankers and Pete Rackley in a breath.

"Yes, it is I," answered the young diver, boldly.

"How did you get here?" demanded Lemuel Hankers, much disconcerted.

"Tumbled."

"Tumbled?"

"That is what I said, Lemuel Hankers. Have you any objection to my being here?"

"You followed us. You have been playing the part of a spy!" cried the rich man.

"How could I have followed you, seeing that I am on this side of the stream?"

"You leaped over."

"No, he couldn't do that, dad," interposed Bart. "He must have come in some other way."

"You overheard our talk?"

"I did."

At this Pete Rackley emitted a low whistle.

"In that case our cake is dough," he muttered.

"Not if I know it," muttered Lemuel Hankers, savagely. "Do you think I am to be worsted by a mere boy?" And he shook his fist at Dave.

All three of the young diver's enemies came to the edge of the stream.

"How did you get where you are?" repeated Lemuel Hankers.

"As I said before, I tumbled."

"You are trying to poke fun at me."

"I was never more serious in my life."

"You think you are smart," put in Bart.

"What I think is none of your business."

"We'll make it our business," burst out Lemuel Hankers, wrathfully. "Come over here, and come instantly."

CHAPTER 11

FACING A JAGUAR

Dave was surprised. He had not dreamed that Lemuel Hankers would carry his high-handedness so openly.

"I cannot come over," he said.

"And why not?"

"I cannot leap the distance."

"Then swim across."

"The current is too strong. Besides, I have no more wish for your company than for the company of that snake which just disappeared."

"Boy, you are a—a young scamp!" burst from Lemuel Hankers' lips.

"Thanks, but I don't wish any of your backhanded compliments, Lemuel Hankers. I am not half as much of a scamp as you are a villain."

"A villain?"

"That's what I said."

"Don't you dare to call my dad names," put in Bart, shaking his fist across the stream.

"I overheard your plot," went on Dave, ignoring Bart. "It's a pretty piece of business for a gentleman to propose."

At this Lemuel Hankers grew red and then pale.

"You—you know too much, boy," he faltered. "Come over here, I say. Or shall I bring you?"

"I don't see how you are going to bring me. You can't get over the stream any better than I can."

"It's running very strong, dad," announced Bart, who had been testing the current with some chips. "I don't believe anybody can get across without a long plank. He must have gotten into the cave from the other end."

"Then we can get in that way, too," put in Pete Rackley. "We ought to make him a prisoner," he added, in a low voice.

"I don't think you will get in," thought Dave. "If you do, the chances are you won't come out alive."

A short talk followed, which Dave could not hear.

Then Pete Rackley left the cave on a run, to reappear a few minutes later with a good-sized tree limb which the storm of a few days before had brought down.

"Now we'll get him!" cried Rackley, and threw the limb over the stream.

Dave was much startled. He knew not what to do, for to retreat was impossible.

Soon Rackley was over the underground stream, and Lemuel Hankers and his son followed.

All three ran after the young diver, who retreated to the extreme rear of the cavern.

Here Rackley caught him by the arm.

"You had better submit quietly," said Rackley. "If you don't, it will be the worse for you."

Dave saw at once that resistance was out of the question.

They were three to one, and all armed, while he was unarmed, and still weak from his tumble and what had followed.

"You have no right to make me a prisoner," he remarked, for the want of something better to say.

"We'll take the right," said Rackley, with a wicked grin. "Didn't expect to see me here, after our little affair in the Washington hotel, did you?" he added.

"Perhaps you'll get left now, as you did then," retorted Dave.

Rackley produced a rope which he had brought in with the tree limb, and soon Dave's hands were bound behind him.

"I have an idea," said Lemuel Hankers. "Why can't we leave him in this cave until both ships have sailed?"

"Just my notion," answered Rackley.

"You can feed him until the *Raven* gets back, and he will be kind of company for you."

"I'll feed him if he behaves himself," growled Pete Rackley.

All three of the others tried their best to "pump" Dave, but could get nothing out of the young diver regarding his father's plans or those of Captain Broadbeam.

"You must find out yourself," he answered.

He was made to march to the extreme right of the cave, and here Rackley fastened him to a sharp rock which jutted from one of the walls.

"There, I reckon he won't get loose from that in a hurry," said the rascal, after his job was finished.

Then the three evildoers withdrew to the mouth of the cave, stopping at the underground stream just long enough to remove the tree limb so that Dave could not cross the stream even if he did get free.

A quarter of an hour later the others went away from the cave, and all became as silent as a tomb.

If the young diver had been disheartened before, he was now utterly cast down.

He was a prisoner of the enemy, and he felt almost certain that Pete Rackley would desert him and leave him to starve.

No food had been left with him excepting that which was in the water-soaked pouch that he carried.

And this he could not get at, for his hands were still bound tightly behind him.

An hour went by, and to him it seemed an age.

His thoughts wandered back to the *Swallow*. How was his stricken father getting along, and what did he think of his disappearance?

And what had become of poor Bob Vilett, who had accompanied him on this ill-fated expedition after game?

"Captain Broadbeam will most likely send out an expedition in search of us," he reasoned, "but I don't think any of them will come in here."

But then his hopes brightened a little.

Perhaps if the captain sent out somebody to look for himself and Bob, that person might discover the *Raven* in that port.

"If the *Raven* is discovered, father will feel sure Lemuel Hankers has had a hand in my disappearance, and he'll take the rascal to task for it."

Dave did not know that Lemuel Hankers had given strict orders to Captain Nesik, of the *Raven*, to keep out of sight of the *Swallow*, and that the *Raven* was now well hidden in a little cove thickly surrounded by palms and tropical vines.

In less than two hours after leaving Dave, Lemuel Hankers and his son rejoined the *Raven*.

"What has become of Pete Rackley?" questioned Captain Nesik.

"He went off by himself," answered Lemuel Hankers. "To my mind, he isn't just right in his head."

"Why, what do you mean?"

"He ran around like a crazy man, and broke out into the wildest kind of singing. Said he was done with living on a ship, and was going to become a hermit."

This story was told for the benefit of the crew of the *Raven*.

In private, Lemuel Hankers told Captain Nesik the truth, and before nightfall the captain went ashore, pretending to look for Rackley.

When he came back he announced that Rackley must be dead, for he had found his hat at the top of a high cliff overlooking the ocean, and a part of his jacket on the jagged rocks below.

That night the *Raven* pulled up anchor and left the vicinity of the island. Before morning she was crowding on all steam, steering straight for the spot where the sunken treasure ship had gone down.

On board of the *Swallow* there was much anxiety when Dave and the engineer did not return.

Captain Broadbeam did not deem it advisable to acquaint Amos Fearless with the true state of affairs at once.

When the old diver asked where Dave was, he was told that his son and Bob Vilett had determined to stay out until the next day.

In the meantime poor Dave remained a prisoner in the cave. His wet clothing gave him something of a chill during the night, and morning found him sick and hungry, and almost ready to give up in despair.

It was scarcely daylight when Dave heard odd-sounding footsteps approaching from the outer entrance of the cave.

He strained his eyes and at last made out a large wild animal.

It was a savage-looking jaguar, and had tracked the footsteps of those who had come to the cave the day before.

Presently the jaguar came to the underground stream.

Here it paused for a moment, then leaped to the other side.

It was now less than fifty yards from where Dave stood, a prisoner.

Suddenly the wild beast lifted its head, stared into the darkness, and gave a growl of rage.

It had discovered the helpless boy!

CHAPTER 12

WELL-TIMED SHOTS

"I am lost now for sure!"

Such were the words which escaped Dave Fearless' lips as he watched the approach of the jaguar that had entered the cave and leaped the underground stream.

The young diver had long since given up trying to loosen the bonds which held him so tightly to the jagged rocks. Pete Rackley had done his villainous work well, and the efforts to get free had only caused the cords to sink deeply into Dave's wrists and ankles, until now the blood was flowing freely from those members.

And it was this blood which the wild beast of the island forest had scented!

The growl of the jaguar echoed and re-echoed throughout the lonely cave, causing Dave to shiver as with the ague.

It did indeed look as if the young diver's last hour on earth had come.

"Hi, go away!" he cried, frantically. "Go away! Scat!"

The cries caused the jaguar to pause while yet fifty feet from the youth.

It had never before attacked a human being, and the new experience caused it to proceed with caution.

But now it advanced again, crouching low on the cavern floor, its two eyes glowing like balls of fire in the semi-darkness of the retreat.

Nearer and nearer came the beast, until Dave imagined he could feel the hot breath of the jaguar upon his cheek. Then the tail of the animal began to oscillate slowly, showing that the jaguar was preparing to make a leap.

Bang! Bang!

Almost deafening was the double report of a repeating rifle as it rang throughout the cave. At the shots the jaguar leaped high in the air, turned over several times, and then stretched itself in a convulsive death shudder.

Dave could scarcely believe his eyes and ears. Who had thus unexpectedly come to his deliverance?

"Bob!" The cry was little short of a scream. "Where in the world did you come from?"

"From the bowels of the earth, I reckon," was the reply, as the young engineer of the *Swallow* ran forward. "Is the beast dead?" he went on, as he halted at the outer edge of the underground stream.

"I guess he is," answered Dave, watching the jaguar for a moment. "You are a good shot."

"I knew I had to kill him, or it would be all up with you, Dave. But how came you to be bound to yonder rock?"

"It's a long story. Take care of that stream, or you'll go underground again. You'll have to get a tree limb, or something, before you can come over. I think you'll find a tree limb at the mouth of the cave."

Without delay Bob Vilett ran out of the cave again, to return in a few minutes with the very tree limb Pete Rackley had used for crossing the stream.

Soon the young engineer was at Dave's side, and a slash or two of a pocket-knife set the young diver free.

Then both lost no time in quitting the cave.

Sitting down near the entrance, each told his story, to which the other listened with close attention.

Bob Vilett had lost his senses after going down into the hole, and had recovered, to find himself resting on a ledge in another cave, not far from the one Dave was occupying.

In trying to get out he had lost his way, and had at last emerged in the middle of a tiny valley choked with brush, vines, and other tropical growth.

He had wandered around until chance had brought him to the cave where Dave was a prisoner, and he had been astonished beyond measure to hear his friend calling loudly.

"It was a lucky thing that I retained my rifle, and that the water didn't hurt the cartridges," concluded Bob. "Had it been otherwise, the jig would have been up with you."

"That's true, Bob, and I shan't forget what you have done for me," returned Dave, warmly.

"Where have the rascals gone?"

"I don't know. Probably they have carried out the plot they mentioned while here."

"Then the *Raven* has sailed."

"But what of the *Swallow*? Surely they wouldn't sail without us."

"I don't think they would. We must hunt her up without delay."

"I must have something to eat first. I am as hungry as—as that jaguar was."

"Hurrah! I have it. Let's broil ourselves a jaguar steak, just for the novelty."

To this Dave instantly agreed, and returning to the cave, they brought the beast forth and Bob proceeded to cut him up.

The steak was soon broiling over a fire which Dave kindled, and the smell proved more than appetizing.

The jaguar meat was tough and not of an extra fine flavor, yet they were tremendously hungry, and that made them less critical than otherwise.

In less than an hour the dinner was over, and after getting a drink and a wash-up, both proceeded on their way.

It was warm outside of the cave, so they did not suffer much inconvenience because of their wet clothing.

"Now to find our way back to the *Swallow*, and with all speed," said Dave. "Which do you suppose is the right direction?"

"That way," and Bob pointed with his hand.

"And I was thinking it was in that direction," and Dave pointed at right angles to the other course.

Then both laughed.

"We can't both be right," said Bob.

"Let us split the difference and take a course between the two. Then we probably won't go far wrong, Bob."

"Right you are."

On they went, into the valley which Bob had traversed, and then up the line of hills where they had shot the goats just after coming ashore.

But now they found themselves confronted by a deep ravine, partly choked with brush and vines.

"How are we going to get across that, Dave?"

"We'll have to walk along the bank until we reach some crossing-place," answered the young diver. "I am not going to risk a tumble by taking a leap."

"Nor I. I have had tumbles enough to last me a lifetime," and the young engineer shook his head dubiously.

On they went, the way growing more perilous every moment. They were at the edge of a forest, and the top of the ravine was lined with loose rocks.

Suddenly Bob, having made a leap from one rock to another, went down in a heap and gave a loud cry of pain.

"My foot! My foot!"

"What's the matter?"

"I've caught my foot under the rock!"

Dave immediately hastened forward, and saw that his chum was indeed fast.

The foot was wedged in a crevice, and could not be budged until Dave rolled the rock away by main force.

Then Bob grated his teeth and gave a deep groan.

"My ankle! It must be broken! Oh, Dave!"

And with another moan he fell back in a faint.

If Dave had been alarmed before, he was doubly so now, and he scarcely knew what to do. He remembered passing a pool of water a distance back, and he ran to this, filling the water bottle Bob had been carrying.

The water revived the young engineer somewhat, and in the meantime Dave cut loose his shoe. He found the injured ankle much discolored, and swelling rapidly. He bathed it, and this gave some relief, until the pain gave way to a stiff numbness.

"Now I am in a pickle," groaned Bob. "Did ever anybody run up against such luck before?"

"Better not try to stand yet," replied Dave.

"Stand? Why, the pain would go to my very heart if I tried it!" And poor Bob gave another groan.

Dave walked back and got more water, and after another bath the sprained ankle was bound up in some crushed leaves and some linen torn from one of the youth's shirtsleeves. Then they made themselves as comfortable as possible on the rocks, and began to talk over the new turn of affairs.

"Do you think I had better go on alone?" questioned Dave.

"I don't know. Somehow, I don't think we ought to separate."

"I agree, and yet we ought to try to reach the *Swallow* as soon as possible."

"That's so, too."

"Supposing I try to get over the ravine and to the top of the hill? I won't get out of rifle shot, and it may be I'll be able to spot our ship from the hilltop."

"All right, go ahead. But don't wander too far, or—gracious, look!"

He broke off short and pointed to a tree growing close at hand.

The leaves of the tree had parted slowly, and now from between them appeared the hideous head and shoulders of a monstrous gorilla! The gorilla's eyes were bent upon both boys, and the beast looked as if he meant immediate mischief!

CHAPTER 13

SURROUNDED BY SAVAGES

"He's coming down on us, Bob!"

"Jump and save yourself, Dave!"

Crack! Bang!

The cries and shots were uttered almost at the same time, and the air was instantly filled with smoke, followed by an unearthly squeal from the gorilla, who instantly disappeared from view.

But the beast was not seriously wounded, for the rifle balls had merely nipped his paw and his shoulder, and he was in a terrible rage.

"Is he dead, Bob?"

"Reckon not, for I can hear him climbing through the tree."

"We ought to get away from here, for there may be more of the gorillas about."

"That's true. But I can't walk."

"I'll carry you."

And having allowed Bob to slip some extra cartridges into the repeating rifle, Dave took his friend up in his arms.

He was just about to start down the ravine when the gorilla showed himself a second time.

He had armed himself with half-green cocoanuts, and taking aim, he let fly at Dave's head.

"Dodge!" yelled Bob, and the cry came none too soon, for the missile brushed over the top of the young diver's head. Then came several more cocoanuts, and Bob was struck in the side.

He could not stand the fusillade, and watching his chance, discharged the rifle again.

He only fired one shot, but this found its way through the gorilla's stomach, and mortally wounded the creature.

Down dropped the cocoanuts, one at a time. Then the animal's hold relaxed, and he too came down, almost at the feet of the youths.

The distorted, half-human face was terrible to look upon, and both Dave and Bob turned quickly away.

"I never want to see another gorilla," shuddered Dave.

"And I never want to shoot one," responded Bob.

Along the ravine went the young diver, carrying his friend upon his shoulder.

Two hundred feet of the rough way was covered when they reached a spot where the ravine might be crossed with ease.

Over they went, and then Dave set down his burden and took a well-earned rest.

By this time night was coming on, and still they were at least half a mile from the seacoast.

"We won't gain the *Swallow* today," murmured the young diver, ruefully.

"And perhaps we won't gain the ship at all," responded the young engineer.

As is usual in the tropics, night came on suddenly. The sun went down behind the trees and the rim of the distant ocean, and soon the stars shone out clearly and beautifully.

All was quiet save for the sounds of the night birds in the thicket behind them.

To keep off the wild animals they built a large camp-fire, and at this cooked some of the meat they had brought along from the cave.

Bob's ankle was cared for several times during the evening, and the youth declared that it now felt much better.

They took turns watching during the night, yet little came to disturb them. Once Dave heard a wild animal approaching and brought up the rifle, ready to fire on the instant. But the fire made the beast keep his distance, and he finally slunk away without showing himself.

Both boys were up at daybreak, and Bob declared that he would try to walk upon his foot, at least as far as the seacoast.

A quarter of an hour's climb took them to the top of the hills, and here they took a good look at the beach and the ocean spread out before them.

Not a sign of the *Swallow* was to be seen anywhere.

This was disheartening, and Dave's heart sank.

Were they really deserted?

"We can't see all of the beach from here," said Bob, encouragingly. "See, yonder patch of wood hides a good stretch from view. The *Swallow* may be behind that. And even if she has gone off, remember that Pete Rackley was to disable her so that she would have to put back for repairs."

"And so far as he was concerned, I might have starved in the meantime," added Dave, bitterly.

"Yes. He must be a thorough rascal."

"He is. But no worse than Lemuel Hankers, to my way of thinking, Bob."

"Right you are."

They had to be careful in descending the side of the hill, for here were many treacherous stones, and neither wished to risk another sprained ankle.

But at last they stood at the bottom, with the ocean's shore but half a dozen rods away.

The foam from the breakers could be seen distinctly through the tall palms, and with their hearts beating rapidly they hurried forward to where a long stretch of dazzling sand stood as a barrier between the woodland and the water.

"No ship here," said Dave, soberly.

"This is not the spot where the *Swallow* cast anchor, Dave. The question is, was that cove north or south of here?"

"North, I should say."

"This time I agree with you. Come, walking along the beach will be easy enough."

And so it proved, although the fierce rays of the sun soon made both more than willing to seek the shade of the overhanging palms and other tropical trees which lined the beach.

At a distance ahead the beach curved, and as they approached this spot they heard a sudden wild shouting, combined with a flapping, which was altogether new to their ears.

"Savages, I'll bet a dollar!" cried Bob. "We had better go into hiding!"

"But what is that other noise?" queried Dave.

"I can't imagine. But come, don't stay here."

Both started for the forest, but the movement came too late.

From around the curve of the beach appeared half a dozen wild savages of the South Sea type, and the two youths were discovered.

"Hi ki werra!" shouted one of the savages. He was armed with a bow and arrows, and quickly leveled an arrow at Dave, who was nearest.

"Hi ki werra!" repeated the other savages, and they, too, leveled their arrows. "The white demons! The white demons!"

"We are in for it now!" whispered Dave.

"Give them a shot from the rifle!"

"No, that would only make them mad," replied the young engineer. Nevertheless, he pointed the rifle at the head of the nearest native.

The effect was magical, for the savage immediately threw up both hands and began to yell like a madman.

He had once seen a gun go off and a goat shot thereby, and he imagined the "white demon" was going to slay him likewise.

The other savages also came to a halt, and all lowered their arrows.

Then Bob lowered the rifle.

A long pause on both sides followed.

The natives did not know what to do, and the youths were in a similar predicament.

One of the savages began to jabber away in his native tongue, but neither Dave nor Bob understood a word of what was said.

"This is all Greek to me!" shouted Dave.

"Talk English."

"Englees!" repeated the savage, and shook his head. He understood that single word, but no more.

"We want to be left alone," put in Bob. "If you don't leave us alone, somebody will get hurt."

"Englees," repeated the native. Then, struck by a sudden inspiration, he advanced a few feet, threw down his bow and arrows, and held out his hands.

"He wants to be friendly, evidently," observed Bob.

"If it isn't a trick," answered the young diver. "I must say I don't like their looks."

"No more do I; but what are we to do, retreat?"

"Rather than fall into the hands of cannibals I'd go back over the hills to the cave."

The native was coming closer, and he tried to put as pleasant a look on his face as possible.

But the effort was a failure, for he was both crafty and cruel, and this disposition shone in every line of his reddish-black features.

"Go back!" shouted Bob, and raised the rifle again.

Scarcely had he spoken when there came a shout from the rear, and looking behind them, the two youths found that they were surrounded!

CHAPTER 14

ANOTHER CAPTURE

"We are in for it now, Dave!"

"Right you are, Bob. What shall we do, fight?"

"It would be useless, for they outnumber us ten to one."

And so speaking, Bob lowered the rifle once more.

It was well he did so, otherwise several arrows would have been sent whizzing through his body.

In a few seconds the natives had closed in on them and taken the rifle and other things from them.

Then they were bound with thongs and carted up the beach.

During all this time the thrashing on the beach ahead had continued, and now the boys saw what caused it.

In some unaccountable manner a whale had become cast up by the breakers.

He was caught in some brushwood and a fallen tree, but was doing his best to get back into his native element.

The savages considered the whale a great find, and were doing all in their power to make him their prisoner and kill him.

Scores of arrows had been shot into the huge, blubbery body, and the beach was dyed crimson with the blood of the marine monster.

Yet he thrashed around lively, and one native who went too near was knocked senseless by a blow from the whale's tail.

The fighting with arrows went on for a quarter of an hour longer, and in the meantime a long rope, made of vines and as tough as rawhide, was passed around the monster and made fast to a tree back of the beach.

The whale fought to the last, but gradually its struggles grew less and less, and finally ceased altogether.

Then arose a loud shouting, and rushing in, the savages began to dig at the body with their long knives and their war hatchets.

Some of the blubber they ate raw, much to the disgust of the prisoners, who found themselves forced to look on.

"They are worse than Esquimaux," muttered Dave. "Ugh! It makes me sick at the stomach."

"I wonder what they intend to do with us?"

"There is no telling. But I guess they won't eat us so long as the whale meat lasts. They seem to relish that immensely."

The boys passed a dismal half-hour, and during that time the savages cut up the whale and carted the meat off in huge chunks.

Then a savage who was evidently a chief came up and ordered some of his followers to bring Dave and Bob along.

Still bound, the two chums were picked up by two savages, who seemed to count their weight as nothing.

A journey lasting over an hour followed, straight into the interior of the island.

At the end of the inland lake previously mentioned, the band of savages halted.

Bob and Dave were tied fast to two trees, and then the natives proceeded to hold a council of war.

They wished to question the lads, but not one of them could speak English.

Presently a loud chanting was heard, and from a distance the boys saw more savages approaching.

There were three men and half a dozen women.

There was likewise another man, but he was white, even though his face had evidently been stained a reddish-brown color.

This man wore an attire which was comical in the extreme.

The suit consisted of a sailor's shirt and trousers, the latter cut off at the knees, and a shiny stovepipe hat, the band filled with feathers.

"Great Scott!" burst from Dave. "Look at that scarecrow!"

As soon as the man in the silk hat appeared all of the natives began bowing and chanting in chorus, and this they kept up until the strange one lifted his hands and let out a peculiar yell.

Then the stranger caught sight of the boys and ran up to them.

"Be th' eyes av Saint Patrick!" he cried, in a rich Irish brogue. "Who are ye, now; tell me that?"

"An Irishman!" said Dave, fervently. "Thank Heaven, one man can talk United States."

"Who are you?" demanded Bob.

At this the Irishman took off the stovepipe, swung it into the air, and made them a profound bow.

"Sure, I am Pat Stoodles, grand muck-a-muck av this wild tribe av hay-thins, castaway sailor from th' bark *Emma D.*, high lord av the island, and second cousin av the royal Emperor of Turkey, ha, ha!"

And he laughed long and loud, and then shook hands.

"Are you putting this on for the natives' benefit?" questioned Bob. "If you are, let me say they don't understand a word."

At once a frown crossed Pat Stoodles' face.

He was indeed a castaway, and a solitary life of several years had partly turned his brain.

When the savages had found him he had acted so strangely that they had fancied he was some inhabitant of the infernal region. At first they had wanted nothing to do with him, but they had ended by making him something of a chief. In their own language they called him the fun-making high lord.

Pat Stoodles listened to their talk with interest, but shook his head when they mentioned the *Swallow*.

"You are afther bein' mistaken about th' ship," he said. "No ship comes here. What looks loike a ship is a vision in th' heavens, nothin' more!" And he clenched his fists. He had looked so long for a sail when alone that the subject had turned his brain.

"Poor chap!" said Bob, in an undertone, "I don't believe he can help us much."

"Perhaps he can save our lives." Our hero turned to the Irishman. "What will these natives do with us!"

"Sure an' I don't know. Maybe they'll be afther makin' princes av ye, me bould b'ys!"

"We would like our liberty."

Pat Stoodles shrugged his shoulders.

"Ye can gain yer liberty on but wan night av the month," he said. "That is whin th' moon is full an' they be afther havin' the feast av the skulls."

They did not know if he was in earnest, or if the talk was that of a crazy man.

Having spoken with them for some time, Pat Stoodles turned to the natives and began to jabber at them.

Evidently he had learned much of their language, for they listened attentively.

Then they brought the boys something to eat and to drink, and tried to make them otherwise comfortable.

But they would allow neither of them his liberty.

Night came and went, and still the chums remained prisoners of the savages.

Pat Stoodles spoke to them a long while in the morning, and at last appeared to believe their story of a ship.

"I will be afther lookin' fer her," he said. "But it's more likely a drame. I used to be afther dramin' loike that meself." And then he disappeared.

The morning slipped by, and the boys were thoroughly miserable. At first the natives left them alone, but presently they came on one after another and pulled their noses, their ears, and their hair. One savage doused them with dirty water from the lake, and all laughed loudly at the trick.

Noon had come and gone, when of a sudden several shots sounded in the distance.

The shots were followed by a loud yelling of natives, and at once those surrounding Dave and Bob ran off to learn the cause of the conflict.

"Something is up!" cried Dave. "What can it mean?"

"I reckon we'll soon learn," answered the young engineer.

A few more shots followed, and soon after all became quiet, the stillness lasting for over an hour.

Then a chanting was heard, and a body of savages appeared, having in their midst two prisoners.

"Look!" cried Dave. "Captain Broadbeam and Doctor Barrell! Is it possible!"

He was right. The newly made prisoners were the captain and the doctor, who had been surprised while on a second hunt for the missing ones.

CHAPTER 15

A DOOR OF WATER

"Dave Fearless! And Bob Vilett! Thank Heaven you are not dead!"

So spoke Captain Broadbeam as his eyes rested upon the two youthful prisoners of the savages.

The captain's clothing was torn, and there were marks of blood upon his face, showing that he had not submitted without a struggle. Indeed, both the captain of the *Swallow* and Doctor Barrell had fought to the bitter end.

"We have been hunting everywhere for you," put in the doctor. "Some thought you dead, but we were not willing to believe it."

"Did a man named Pete Rackley come to the *Swallow*?" questioned Dave, quickly.

"I know nothing of a man of that name," answered the captain, "but there came to us a poor and forlorn castaway, who said he had been alone on this island for nearly two years."

"Please describe him," said Bob.

The captain did so. Both Dave and Bob gave a groan.

"He is a fraud!" burst out the young diver.

"And he will wreck the *Swallow* before we can get back to her," added Bob.

Of course, both Captain Broadbeam and Doctor Barrell were astonished at these remarks.

"I don't understand," said the master of the ship.

As quickly as he could Dave explained the plot which had been hatched out by Lemuel Hankers and which Rackley, his tool, was to carry out.

"It is dastardly!" cried both the captain and the doctor.

"And to think I took him on board, gave him new clothing, and promised him pay until we should get back to the States," added the captain.

"Even now he may be wrecking my beautiful engine!" groaned Bob. "Oh, if only I had the rascal by the neck!"

The savages now interrupted the talk by separating the prisoners, tying each to a tree some distance from the others.

Pat Stoodles was nowhere to be seen, for he had gone off in an entirely different direction from that taken by the natives.

Slowly the day dragged by until night was at hand. The natives were busy preparing the meat taken from the whale, and for the time being paid but scant attention to the prisoners.

"We must escape tonight," thought Dave.

Yet how was it to be accomplished?

Although the natives took little notice of them, one of the younger men of the tribe had been set on guard, to see that none of them broke his bonds.

At last darkness settled down on the encampment. At first the fire blazed brightly, but at last it died down, leaving the prisoners in gloom.

The savages gathered close to the camp-fire, the women by themselves, and were soon wrapped in slumber.

One native remained on guard, seated on a fallen tree.

Suddenly a form appeared in the midst of the prisoners.

It was Pat Stoodles, but so transformed that Dave scarcely recognized the half-witted Irish castaway.

Stoodles was dressed in a suit of skins, and on his head rested a crown made of horn, set with peacock feathers.

In his hand the Irishman carried a long knife.

"I am the King of the Island Windjammers!" he cried, in a low tone. "I am sent to free the world! Avaunt, ye ghosts of ships! Begone, ye rats of my brain! Ha! And how is that, my bonnie b'y! An' that! An' that!"

Rambling on in this fashion, he quickly cut the ropes which held Dave and Bob. Then he turned to Captain Broadbeam and of a sudden he stopped with mouth wide open.

"Captain Broadbeam, or is it another av thim drames?" he gasped.

"Pat Stoodles!" cried the captain. "And so you are the king of these savages. Release me at once!"

"I will! I will!" answered Stoodles, and cut the bonds, and also those of the doctor.

All this time the savage on guard was looking on in silence, for he dared not interfere with the doings of Stoodles. Yet he grew uneasy when he saw all the prisoners liberated and saw the Irishman shake Captain Broadbeam by the hand. He gave a sudden and shrill cry.

Quick as a flash Stoodles turned upon him.

"That's fer ye!" roared the Irishman, and knocked him flat with a blow of his fist.

"Quick, we must get away!" cried Dave. "See, all of the savages are awake!"

He spoke the truth, and the others felt that they must fly on the instant or it would be too late.

"To the woods!" cried the doctor. "Perhaps we can hide!"

"I will show ye a spot!" put in Stoodles. "I have a cave all me own where they won't be afther findin' ye!"

He led the way and the others followed, through the brush and up a hill back of the lake upon which the encampment was located.

It was a crooked and dangerous path, yet by keeping close to Stoodles they avoided many a nasty pitfall.

Soon they heard the savages on their trail. At first they were some distance off, but gradually they grew closer and closer.

"I can't go much further!" gasped poor Bob. "My ankle pains me something awful!"

"Don't ye be afther givin' up!" said Pat Stoodles. "We'll soon be at me castle, which all the savages on the island can't conquer."

They were now passing along the bed of a small stream which flowed into the lake. Presently before them arose a beautiful waterfall, twenty feet high and eight or nine feet broad.

"That's the dure av me castle," announced Stoodles. "Make a quick sthep inside an' ye'll not git overly wet."

With this he dove straight into the waterfall and disappeared from view.

"Gracious! What does that mean?" came from Dave.

"He is mad and has committed suicide," muttered the doctor.

"Perhaps not," came from Bob. "That waterfall may conceal the entrance to a cave."

"Hurrah! I believe you are right," answered Dave. "And I am for finding out," and he took a step forward.

But the captain caught the young diver by the shoulder.

"Don't be rash, lad. It may cost you your life."

Scarcely had Captain Broadbeam spoken when Stoodles reappeared through the falling sheet of water.

"Come on!" he cried. "Don't be afraid. The futtin' is safe enough," and again he disappeared.

None of the others hesitated any longer. Dave went first, holding his breath as he took the plunge. To his surprise the falling body of water was less than four inches thick, and in a moment he found himself on a smooth, rocky floor.

"That's the greatest yet!" muttered Bob, when all were safe in the cave under the upper stream. "Don't the savages know of this?" he asked of the Irishman.

"Sure not. Once they followed me up the strame an' I scared the wits out av thim, talkin' to thim from the wathers!" And Pat Stoodles laughed loudly, a laugh that echoed and re-echoed throughout the cavern.

It was pitch-dark, but soon they had a light, and Stoodles brought forth a torch.

Then he led the way to a branch of the cave, on higher ground.

Here the flooring and walls were perfectly dry, and here the castaway had something of a comfortable home, with a rude table, a bench, a sea chest, and a cupboard with dishes and other household articles.

In one corner of the cave was a rough fireplace, the smoke of a fire going up through half a dozen small cracks.

It was easy to see that the castaway had not always been simple-minded.

"I knew him years ago quite well," said Captain Broadbeam. "He once sailed under me. He is suffering for the want of companionship. Many a castaway, you know, has gone stark mad through loneliness. The savages were really no company for him."

"Do you think he will get over it?" asked Dave.

"I think he will," put in the doctor. "I have seen such cases before. Sometimes the recovery is quite rapid, when the castaway gets back among his own people."

Leaving the crowd seated around a comfortable fire, in order to dry their clothing before going to sleep, Pat Stoodles returned to the entrance of the cave.

He was gone the best part of half an hour, when he returned in considerable excitement.

"The haythins have tracked us to the waterfall!" he whispered. "An' wan av thim—Chief Walru—is thinkin' av thryin' to git behind th' water into the cave!"

CHAPTER 16

THE ESCAPE TO THE COAST

The announcement that the savages were trying to get into the cave under the waterfall filled Dave and his friends with new alarm.

"You are sure of this, Stoodles?" questioned Captain Broadbeam, as he leaped to his feet.

"I am," was the Irishman's answer.

"We ought to be able to hold them back," put in the doctor. "Can't we hurl them into the stream as fast as they appear?"

"That's the talk," came from Bob. "Let us line up just this side of the waterfall."

"Perhaps we can scare them," suggested Dave. "I know all savages are very superstitious."

All made their way to the edge of the waterfall, and Pat Stoodles showed them a crack in the rocks, at the side of the falls.

Here they could see the savages lined up outside, with Chief Walru at their head.

Several were talking excitedly, and the chief was wading in the water at the very foot of the falls.

Now the chief took up a rock and hurled it into the waterfall.

It whizzed past Doctor Barrell and struck the flooring some distance to the rear of the cave.

Dave saw the movement, and of a sudden a strange idea came into his head.

He would scare the savages if he could.

Filling his lungs with air, he let out a most blood-curdling scream, followed by a series of wild and unearthly groans and a long hiss.

The savages were thunderstruck, and those on the bank of the stream took to their heels with all possible speed, while Chief Walru tumbled backward and then began to scramble over the rocks for dear life.

Again Dave let out a scream, and then groans which were more dreadful than the others.

In less than three minutes not a savage was to be seen.

"They have gone!" said Bob.

"If only they don't come back," returned Captain Broadbeam.

"I have an idea," said the young diver. "Why can't we pile up some stones in front of that opening? Then if the savages try to get through the waterfall they will get badly left."

"That's the talk!" came from Bob. "Are there stones handy, Stoodles?"

"Sure, plinty of thim."

And the Irishman showed the way to where lay a quantity of stones, large and small.

With the doctor holding a torch to light them, all hands began to haul stones to the opening. Those that were flat were placed on the bottom and soon the opening was filled up to within two feet of the top. Other stones were piled up behind, so that those in front might not be shoved back.

"Now we are safe—at least for the time being," said Captain Broadbeam. "But the next question is, how are we to escape and get on board of the *Swallow*?"

"Isn't there another exit from the cave?" asked the doctor.

Pat Stoodles shook his head.

"If there is, I never was afther findin' wan," he remarked.

All were utterly worn out by their adventures and by the work on the stone wall, and glad enough to rest.

Yet each took his turn, at a two hours' watch, so that they might not be surprised.

But the savages did not come back during the night, nor did they see anything of the natives during the morning.

Pat Stoodles had provisions stored in the cave and they made a hearty breakfast, after which all felt decidedly better.

From the Irishman, who seemed to be growing clearer in his mind every hour, they learned that they were about half a mile from the seacoast.

The way to the shore lay through a thick jungle, with here and there a treacherous swamp.

With extreme caution they left the cave and started up the stream and into the jungle.

They were constantly on the lookout for the savages, but a quarter of a mile was covered and not a native showed himself.

"Dave scared them for fair," said Bob. "Perhaps they have left the island altogether."

"Don't be afther foolin' yerself," answered Pat Stoodles. "Thim haythins is wust whin they are sthill."

In this remark the Irishman was correct, for hardly had he spoken when an arrow whizzed through the air and pierced Doctor Barrell's hat.

"They are after us!" cried several in chorus.

"We must run fer it!" came from Stoodles. "Folly me, an' be amazin' quick about it, too," and away he leaped at top speed.

Nobody needed a second warning, and all kept as close to the Irishman's heels as possible. He led them into a thicket of vines and underwood. In the meantime several more arrows came flying through the air, and Dave was struck in the shoulder.

"I am hit!" he murmured, and stopped short.

"Is it bad?" asked Captain Broadbeam, who was close to him.

"I—I guess not. But it doesn't feel very good," and the young diver gave a gasp for breath.

As quickly as he could the captain extracted the arrow, and when they were in the thicket the wound was bound up. It was not serious, but it gave Dave a stiff side for several days afterward.

Once the thicket was gained, Pat Stoodles did not halt, but led the way deeper and deeper into the jungle. Some rocks were passed and then they came out on what looked like the edge of a moss-covered opening.

"Stop!" yelled the Irishman at Bob, who was going ahead. "Stop, if ye value yer loife!"

"What's wrong now?" asked the young engineer.

"That spot is afther bein' worse nor the bogs av ould Ireland," explained Pat Stoodles. "It's as sticky as glue. Perhaps we can lead the savages into it."

He led the way around the opening and all followed, pausing on the opposite side.

At that moment the body of natives appeared, and, seeing the whites, broke into a triumphant yell.

A shower of arrows were sent forth, but the whites ran for the shelter of the nearest trees and nobody was struck.

Then out into the opening rushed the savages, still yelling and brandishing their bows and arrows.

But they did not go far.

Less than a rod of the opening was passed when they began to sink into the black ooze beneath the green moss.

They tried to turn back, but it was in vain.

From their ankles they sank to their knees, and then to their waists.

Their war cries changed to shrieks of alarm and then to frantic appeals to their comrades to help them.

Over a dozen were caught in the glue-like bog, and every one of the number was in danger of losing his life.

The whites were totally forgotten, and the others, coming up, turned their whole attention to rescuing those in such dire peril.

Pat Stoodles laughed loud and long over the success of his ruse.

"Now it's good-bye to ye!" he cried, shaking his fist at the natives. "I'm no more the grand muck-a-muck, but a dacent Irish sailor come back to his siven senses."

Again he led the way through the jungle, striking out directly for the ocean shore.

To force their way through the tropical growth was not easy, and made every one of the party pant for breath.

They stirred up many tropical birds and once came upon a colony of monkeys, who fled, shrieking and chattering, in all directions.

At last they could plainly hear the booming of the surf.

"The ocean!" cried Dave.

"If only we come in sight of the *Swallow*!" put in Bob.

"Perhaps we had better be careful before we show ourselves," remarked Captain Broadbeam. "There may be natives on the beach."

The matter was talked over, and it was decided that Stoodles and the captain should go forward to investigate.

The pair were gone less than ten minutes when Captain Broadbeam came running back in excitement.

"The *Swallow* is not in sight," he said.

"But another ship is."

"Another ship?" queried Dave, and then seeing an odd look on the captain's face, he added: "You don't mean the *Raven*?"

"Yes, I do mean the *Raven*!" was the answer, which filled the others with dismay.

CHAPTER 17

A DASH FOR A ROWBOAT

The *Raven* and not the *Swallow* was in sight!

The several members of the party looked at each other questioningly.

What was to be done now?

"I'm sure I'm not going to ask Lemuel Hankers for help," said Dave, decidedly. "I'd rather put up with the savages."

"No! No! That would be foolish," put in Doctor Barrell. "Why, if those natives got hold of us now they would kill us on the spot."

"An' be afther eatin' ye in the bargain," added Pat Stoodles.

"But to go aboard the enemy's ship!" protested the young diver.

"They wouldn't dare to kill us," said Captain Broadbeam.

"They will have to transfer us to our own vessel," said the doctor.

While they were discussing the situation, Stoodles went back to learn what the savages were doing.

Presently he ran up with the information that the natives had divided into two parties, one to help those in the morass and the other to continue the pursuit of the whites.

"An' the second party is afther comin' up fast," he concluded. "Ye must run fer it or invite capture."

"Come, we will join the *Raven* and trust to luck," said Captain Broadbeam. And so it was decided, although against Dave's wishes.

Soon they were out on the beach and running for the cove where the *Raven* lay at anchor.

The ship had gone into hiding to escape being discovered by those on board the *Swallow*.

Lemuel Hankers felt certain that Pete Rackley would so disable Captain Broadbeam's craft that the *Swallow* would never reach the spot where the sunken treasure lay, at the bottom of the Pacific.

Lemuel Hankers was on deck with his son when the party came into sight of the ship.

He gazed intently at the group of running persons who were waving their hands, frantically, toward the ship.

"Give me a glass!" he cried, quickly.

The powerful marine glass belonging to Captain Nesik was handed to him.

He gave one look, then muttered an imprecation not to be placed upon these pages.

"Who is it?" questioned Bart.

"Dave Fearless, Captain Broadbeam and some others, probably men from the *Swallow*!"

"What!" said the youth. "And look, they act as if they wanted to board our ship!"

"They must have learned of Pete Rackley's doings!" burst from Lemuel Hankers' lips, and his face grew deadly pale.

"Then our jig is up, dad."

"They wish to make trouble!" groaned the rich man.

"I wouldn't let them on board," put in Bart, quickly. "Let us pretend not to see them and sail away."

"We'll do it," answered the father.

He ran to where Captain Nesik stood, and gave the necessary order.

The anchor was hove apeak in double-quick order, and the command was passed to the engine room to back the *Raven*, full speed.

Fortunately for the evildoers, steam was up, and in less than half a minute the *Raven* had left the cove and was moving swiftly out into the Pacific Ocean.

Those on shore could scarcely believe their eyes.

"She is sailing away!" burst from Captain Broadbeam.

"They do not intend to take us on board!" put in Doctor Barrell.

"But do they know who we are?" questioned Bob.

"They must know," said Dave. "Remember, they have powerful glasses on board. Perhaps they spotted us as soon as we came into sight."

"It would please them, I suppose, to have the savages kill us," went on the captain. "I wouldn't have believed it before, but I do now—since you have told me what this Pete Rackley was to do."

In bitter disappointment the crowd ran down to the very edge of the cove, Pat Stoodles at their heels.

They saw a number of persons standing on the stern deck of the *Raven*, but could distinguish no faces.

In less than half an hour the ship was far out to sea.

While the party on the beach was watching the receding ship, Stoodles uttered a cry.

"The savages. They be afther coming on again, bad cess to 'em!"

The Irishman was right. The savages had found their trail and were once again after them hot-footed.

Which way now? That was the question in the mind of every member of the party.

It was Dave who solved the problem. Gazing across the cove, he espied a good-sized rowboat half hidden among some bushes.

The boat had been left there by those on the *Raven* the night before, and in the excitement of the departure had been completely forgotten.

"A boat! A boat!" he cried. "Come!"

He led the way on a run, with the others close upon his heels.

But to circle the cove, which was surrounded with tropical trees, vines, and sharp rocks, was not easy; and before half the distance was covered they heard the cries of the savages.

"They are coming closer!" came from Bob. "Perhaps we had better hide again."

"Don't ye be afther doin' such a foolish thing," answered Pat Stoodles. "They kin track ye quicker nor an Indian could do th' thrick. Take to the boat—it's safer."

On they went, over the rocks and through the tangle of undergrowth. Often one or another would stumble, and scratches and rent clothing were numerous. Closer and closer came the natives. When the latter saw how fresh the trail was they let out a blood-curdling cry of triumph.

At last our friends were within a hundred yards of the boat. But now poor Bob was exhausted, for his foot still pained him greatly.

"I—I can't run any—any more!" he gasped.

"Then we'll carry you," answered Captain Broadbeam, and caught the young engineer up in his arms.

At last the rowboat was gained and they were delighted to note that it contained two pairs of stout oars. Into the craft they tumbled as rapidly as possible, and it was Dave who helped Captain Broadbeam to shove off.

The movement came none too soon, for scarcely were all but poor Bob seated at the oars than the natives burst into view through the jungle back of the stretch of beach surrounding the cove.

"Hi gi! We-ra!" they yelled, and then a shower of arrows was aimed at our friends. One arrow cut through the captain's coat and another buried itself in the stern of the rowboat.

"Pull! Pull!" shouted Dave.

And then they all pulled as never before, Captain Broadbeam giving the stroke, and soon the rowboat was carried a hundred feet from shore. But now came a second flight of arrows and Pat Stoodles was hit in the back.

"I'm done fer!" he moaned, and fell in a heap at the bottom of the craft.

"Give me his oar!" came from Bob, and with his teeth set grimly, he caught up the drifting blade and took his place among the rowers.

Shower after shower of arrows now flew all around the rowboat and its occupants and nearly all on board were struck, although none seriously, for the distance was now too great for the savages' aim.

"Keep it up—we'll soon be out of range," panted Captain Broadbeam, and straight out into the broad Pacific plunged the rowboat, over the breakers and then into the mighty swells beyond.

At last the cove began to fade from view and the arrows no more reached them.

"We are saved!" murmured Bob, and then fell unconscious beside Pat Stoodles.

Leaving Dave to continue rowing, that the boat might not be upset by the long ocean swells, Captain Broadbeam and Doctor Barrell turned their attention to Bob and to Pat Stoodles.

It was found that Bob was suffering from a wound in the shoulder, and the loss of blood, following his former weakness, had been too much for him.

"He'll be all right after a while," said the doctor, after binding up the wound. "That is, unless there was poison on the arrow tip, and I see no evidence of such poison in the appearance of any of our wounds."

Poor Pat Stoodles was worse off and it was a grave question whether he would live or die.

He did not regain consciousness, although the doctor did his best for the poor Irishman.

"He needs stimulants," said Doctor Barrell.

"And we haven't so much as a drink of water," answered Captain Broadbeam, soberly.

An hour went by and the hot sun poured down fiercely upon those in the rowboat.

They knew not which way to turn, fearing that if they attempted to land again the savages would follow them up.

"We will row in the direction of the landing place where we first came ashore," said Captain Broadbeam, and this was done.

An hour later Dave let out a cry of dismay.

"The savages! They are after us again!"

He was right. Around a distant point of land had appeared at least a dozen savages, and all were making for the rowboat with all speed!

CHAPTER 18

ON THE BOSOM OF THE OCEAN

"We can't land here!" cried Dave.

"You are right," answered Captain Broadbeam. "See, more savages are coming from behind yonder trees."

"What shall we do?" questioned the doctor, his face full of concern.

"There is but one thing to do—put to sea again," came from the master of the *Swallow*.

The savages came on with a rush, yelling at the top of their lungs. As they approached the water's edge they let fly a shower of arrows. But fortunately for our friends, all fell short of the mark.

As quickly as it could be accomplished, the rowboat was turned around and headed once more from the island. All who had been rowing were tired, but did their best to get the craft away from the shore.

As soon as the savages saw the boat leaving they set up another yell, and several rushed away to find those who were out in the canoes.

But the latter were on the other side of the island, and before they could be notified our friends had, for the time being, made good their escape.

Dave was all but exhausted, and at last dropped his oar and sank in a heap on the seat.

"Played out, eh?" came from Captain Broadbeam. "Well, I don't wonder. I'm about played out myself."

An hour went by and the rowboat rose and fell on the broad swells of the Pacific Ocean.

In vain they looked in all directions for the *Swallow*. The vessel was not to be seen.

All in the rowboat were exceedingly thirsty and would have given much for a drink of water.

Crouched on the seats, with poor Bob and Pat Stoodles beside them, Dave, the captain, and the doctor talked the situation over.

"We are certainly in a pickle," said Dave. "If we can't find the ship, what then?"

"We must find the *Swallow*," declared Captain Broadbeam. "Unless we do, we'll starve to death."

"We might return to the island at nightfall," said the doctor. "Remember, we need water and so do these poor sufferers." And he pointed to Bob and the Irishman.

"That's a scheme," cried Dave. "We might land under cover of darkness and hide somewhere until we can locate the ship."

Slowly the day wore away. Towards nightfall the wind began to blow strongly, sending the spray flying in all directions.

"We can't stand this," was Dave's comment. "If it blows any harder, we'll be swamped."

"We must take to the oars and keep the boat up to the seas," said the captain, and this was done.

A little later it began to rain. At first it did not amount to much, but presently it began to pour. As best they could, they gathered a small quantity of the water and drank it greedily. They also gave Bob and Stoodles a drink, which did the injured much good.

At last night was upon them, black and threatening. The rowboat was drifting in the wind and the rain, but where to none could tell.

"We must take what comes," said Captain Broadbeam, gravely. "We are in the hands of Providence."

Dave was so exhausted he could not keep his eyes open and soon he went sound asleep, and not long after this the doctor followed his example. Only the captain remained awake and he was so exhausted he could do absolutely nothing.

It was about three o'clock in the morning when the wind began to blow a regular hurricane. The mad plunging and pitching of the rowboat aroused Dave.

"What's up?" he cried.

"The storm is increasing," answered the captain.

"Are we still out on the ocean?"

"Yes."

Captain Broadbeam had scarcely spoken when there came a shock that almost turned the rowboat over.

"We have struck!"

"We are going to the bottom!"

The shock aroused all but Pat Stoodles. Bob would have gone overboard had it not been for Dave, who caught the unconscious man by the shoulder and held him.

"Don't—don't hurt me!" groaned Bob. "Oh!"

A moment later came another shock. Then the rowboat appeared to slide over a sand bar, and of a sudden Captain Broadbeam felt the limb of a tree brush his side.

"Hullo! What's this?" he said. "A tree limb—and here's another! Can it be a floating tree—"

"Hurrah! Here's land!" burst out Dave, peering into the darkness. "A shore of some kind."

"Beware of the savages," cautioned Doctor Barrell. "They may be close at hand."

"I'd rather meet the savages than drown in this storm," came bluntly from Captain Broadbeam.

The rowboat had indeed drifted to some sort of a shore. Close at hand was a sandy beach, and beside this some rocks and a grove of tropical trees. The details of the scene were lost in the darkness.

As the rowboat struck on the beach the captain leaped out and hauled the craft up. But he was not quick enough to escape the breakers and one swept over the craft, nearly drowning all on board. Then Dave sprang out, and at last the pair had the boat out of the reach of the sea.

"Thank Heaven we have landed somewhere," declared the youth. "I thought sure we were bound for Davy Jones's locker."

The rowboat was dragged along the beach and the captain, the doctor, and Dave succeeded in turning it over on some rocks, thus making of it a sort of shelter from the storm. Under it they placed Bob and the Irishman, making them as comfortable as circumstances permitted. This done, the three found something of a shelter under the trees and there sank down to rest until morning.

When Dave opened his eyes the sun was shining brightly and close at hand a number of tropical birds were singing gayly. For the moment he could not remember what had occurred and he sat up, gazing around in bewilderment.

"We are shipwrecked," he murmured at length. "I wonder if those savages are anywhere near?"

He arose and stretched himself and then walked out on the shore of the island. None of the others were awake, and he determined to let them rest as long as they wished, providing no danger was at hand.

Not a soul was in sight and the place looked much different from that where the savages had been encountered.

"It looks to me as if this is another island," he reasoned, and he was right.

On the shore were a number of oysters and clams, and he lost no time in picking up as many as he thought they might use for a meal. Then he caught up several stones and sticks and went after the birds. He was good at throwing and soon brought down three birds of fair size.

"Hullo, what's doing?" was the cry, and he saw Captain Broadbeam approaching.

"I'm trying to gather something for breakfast."

"Good enough. Seen anything of the savages?"

"No."

"This doesn't look like the same island."

"Just what I think, captain."

"Well, I hope there are no savages here. Seen anything of the *Swallow*?"

"Nothing whatever."

Some brushwood and sticks were gathered, and after a little trouble a fire was started. The smell of the cooking clams and oysters aroused the others.

"Ha! A fire and breakfast!" cried the doctor. "That interests me!"

"How do you feel, Bob?" questioned Dave, bending over his friend.

"Tired all over, Dave. Where are we?"

"On one of these islands of the ocean."

"Have we escaped from the savages?"

"For the present, yes."

"I'm mighty hungry."

"You shall have breakfast as soon as it is cooked."

"Sure an' I'm hungry meself," came from Pat Stoodles.

"How are you feeling?" questioned the doctor.

"Loike I had been through a clothes wringer, docthor," was the answer. "Bad cess to thim savages!"

Not long after this the clams and oysters, as well as the birds, were ready for eating, and Bob and the Irishman were given what the doctor thought was best for them. The others ate their fill, and after the repast was over all felt much better.

"There are just two things for us to do," said Captain Broadbeam: "Keep out of the way of the savages and find the *Swallow*."

"And in the meantime we have got to feed ourselves and take care of the wounded," added Doctor Barrell.

The matter was talked over and it was decided that the doctor should remain with Bob and Stoodles, while the captain and Dave went on a short tour of exploration.

"I do not imagine that this island is very large," said the captain, as he and Dave set out. "To my mind it won't be a bad idea to skirt the shore first."

"Just as you say," answered the youth.

"We want to keep our eyes peeled for the savages, though."

It was an easy matter to follow the shore on two sides of the island, but to the north and the west were numerous rocks, and they climbed over these only with the greatest difficulty.

"Be careful, or you'll sprain an ankle," said the captain.

"There seems to be a hill near the center of the island," said the young diver. "Wouldn't it be a good idea to climb to the top of that?"

"Yes, as soon as we have finished skirting the shore."

Presently they came to a spot where some extra high rocks hid what was beyond from their view.

"Hark!" cried Dave, coming to a sudden halt. "What was that?"

"I don't know," answered the captain. "Sounded like somebody calling, didn't it?"

Both listened, and presently from the other side of the rocks came a low whine, followed by a scream.

"Somebody is there!" murmured Dave. "Perhaps a savage!"

"We'll take a peep," began Captain Broadbeam, when of a sudden a hairy form leaped on top of the rocks and confronted them.

The form was that of a gorilla. The creature was all of four feet high, with strong limbs and a face of peculiar ferocity.

"Look out!" yelled Dave. "He means mischief!"

The young diver was right. The gorilla gave a snarl, and the next instant made a leap for Captain Broadbeam's shoulder. It landed fairly and squarely on the captain and bore that individual to the ground.

CHAPTER 19

FIGHTING A GORILLA

The appearance of the gorilla had been so unexpected that for the instant Dave knew not what to do. As the captain went down with the creature on top of him, the young diver fancied that the man would surely be killed.

"Help!" cried Captain Broadbeam, and this call aroused the youth to his senses. Catching up a stick, he hit the gorilla a resounding whack on the head. Then he struck at the beast's body.

The gorilla did not like such treatment, and with a snarl it dropped its hold on the captain and turned towards Dave. A moment later it was on the young diver's breast and Dave was doing his utmost to throw the creature off.

It was now the young diver's turn to call for assistance, which he did most lustily.

"I'll help you!" cried the captain, and catching up a stone, he hit the gorilla in the side with it. The creature gave a snarl and sprang back to the top of the rocks. Then it disappeared as suddenly as it had come.

"Ugh!" murmured Dave. "What a horrid beast!"

"Are you hurt?"

"Only a scratch or two."

"We were lucky to get off so easily, lad."

"Is he gone for good?" asked Dave, with a slight shiver.

"I'm sure I don't know."

Each now lost no time in arming himself with a stout club and with a couple of fair-sized and sharp stones. They listened, but could hear nothing of the gorilla.

"I'd feel safer if I knew that beast was dead," said the captain. "He may take it into his head to attack us again."

"And he may be only one of a regular tribe," put in Dave.

"No, Dave; gorillas don't live together like monkeys. At the most you'll find two together."

With great caution they climbed to the top of the rocks and peered over. Not a living creature of any sort was in sight.

"He has gone, that's certain," said Dave, and gave a sigh of relief.

They went on their way, and inside of an hour had walked completely around the island, which was not over half a mile in diameter.

"Now we'll go up the hill and take a look around," said Captain Broadbeam.

On the side of the hill the tropical growth was thick, and they had to fairly cut their way through the tangle of underbrush and long trailing vines.

"This is what I call work," said Dave, panting. "How much further have we to go?"

"Not very much further, Dave. I think—listen!" The captain broke off short and both listened. But only the murmur of the breeze through the trees came to their ears.

"What did you hear?" asked the young diver.

"I fancied I heard that gorilla again."

"Oh, don't say that!"

"Perhaps I was mistaken. But it would be just like the beast to follow us," continued the master of the *Swallow*.

"We will have to be on our guard."

Both looked around with care, but could see nothing of the gorilla. Then they pushed on once more, up the rocks and through a tangle of vines until they reached a bit of a clearing on the very top of the hill.

"Here we are, safe and sound!" said the captain. "I wish we had a spyglass."

They took a careful look around, and noted that the island was circular in form, with a small cove on the south shore, where the rowboat had landed.

On all sides stretched the rolling Pacific, the waves glistening brightly in the strong sunshine.

Not another island of any sort was in sight.

"I believe that other island is to the westward of this," said the captain. "But it's too far off to be located with the naked eye."

"I don't see anything of the *Swallow*, or of any other ship," came from Dave, after he had gazed around for several minutes.

"The ship is probably in the vicinity of that other island."

From the top of the hill they could see that the island was uninhabited. Whether or not any wild beasts outside of the gorilla were located there they could not determine.

"I hope we don't have to stay here too long," remarked the young diver, as they started back for the spot where they had left Bob and Stoodles.

"We'll have to stay until we find the ship."

Halfway down the side of the hill Captain Broadbeam gave a sudden leap into the air.

"Look out!" he screamed.

"What's the matter?" queried Dave.

"Spiders! As big as your hand!"

The master of the *Swallow* was right. He had stepped on a mound which was a spiders' nest, and out from the soil issued ten or a dozen big brown and yellow spiders, most ferocious in their appearance.

The creatures made after both the captain and Dave, and both lost no time in putting a good distance between themselves and that vicinity.

"Gosh! I never saw such spiders in my life!" gasped Dave, when he thought himself safe.

"They certainly were large, Dave. But such things grow big in the tropics."

"They looked as if they might be poisonous."

"They are. We must watch out for them in the future."

Not long after this they came to a spot where a number of bushes were growing, covered with large, oval-shaped berries.

"These berries are perfectly good and very nourishing," said the captain. "Let us pick a quantity and take them back to the camp."

Back of the patch of berries was a fine spring and here they procured a cold drink of water. Just below the spring was a wide pool several feet deep, and in this pool numerous small lizards were darting around.

"Everything is full of life in the tropics," remarked the young diver. "Just look at the birds and fish, and lizards and spiders, and a hundred and one other things!"

"Yes, and the vegetation is very plentiful," added the captain.

They were still some distance from the shore when Dave called a halt.

"Look at the big birds yonder," he whispered. "Can't we bring down two or three with sticks or stones? They will make fine eating."

"We can try it, Dave."

Sticks and stones were handy, and arming themselves they approached a large tree upon which the birds were resting.

"Ready?" asked Dave.

"Yes."

"Throw!"

The youth let fly a short stick and the captain a sharp stone. Down came two birds, one dead and the other seriously wounded. The others set up a wild squawking and flew away.

"Not so bad!" cried the captain, and ran to dispatch the wounded bird.

As he stooped over the bird there was a strange cry from another tree close by and then a whir through the air.

"The gorilla!" said Dave. "Look out!"

The young diver's cry came too late. Down came the beast that had attacked them before, landing directly on Captain Broadbeam's shoulder and clutching the man by the throat!

For the instant Dave was almost paralyzed. But then he realized the captain's peril and rushed in to the man's assistance.

In his hands the young diver clutched a heavy stick, and this he brought down with all force on the gorilla's head.

The creature was taken by surprise and dropped its hold. But its skull was too thick to mind greatly the blow which had been delivered, and an instant later it leaped forward once more, this time for Dave.

The young diver dodged, and in a twinkling the gorilla had Dave around the waist while the youth had the creature around the shoulder and neck. Then began the struggle, the beast trying to bite and Dave trying his best to prevent such a movement.

In the midst of the mêlée Captain Broadbeam rushed to the rescue. He had picked up Dave's stick, which the young diver had dropped, and now he struck the gorilla twice across the back and then across the lower limbs.

Not knowing what to make of this last attack, the creature turned once more and dropped its hold of Dave. But at another blow from the stick it began to retreat, and soon was lost to sight in the jungle on the hillside.

"He has gone!" said the captain, breathing heavily from his exertions.

"What a fighter he is!" gasped Dave. He had all he could do to catch his breath.

"I wish we had killed him, lad. Then he couldn't bother us again."

"Yes, it's too bad we didn't finish him. He will probably lay low for us now. Maybe he'll attack us while we sleep."

"We'll have to stand guard."

Making certain that the gorilla had really left the vicinity, they continued the journey to the shore, reaching the camp a little while later. They found Doctor Barrell waiting impatiently for their return. Both Bob and the Irishman were sleeping soundly.

"And what did you discover?" asked the man of science.

"Very little," answered the captain. "But we have had a couple of nasty fights."

"With the savages?"

"No, with a gorilla."

"Is it possible! Did you kill the creature?"

"No, he got away."

"Too bad! I would give much to catch a gorilla alive. We could add him to our collection."

"Thanks, but no live gorilla in mine," came promptly from Dave. "Give me a dead one every time."

The doctor listened to their story with much interest and was glad to see they had brought some berries and the birds for a meal.

"I have found some herbs and plants and given both of the sufferers medicine," said he. "I think Bob Vilett will recover rapidly, but it will take time to bring Pat Stoodles around."

It was now midday, and the sun was scorching. This being so, all were content to rest in the shade. A fire was built, and over it the birds and also some oysters were done to a turn, and these, with the berries, made a good meal for all.

During the afternoon Dave made himself a good bow and also several arrows. The captain followed his example, and also cut several good-sized clubs.

"We must arm ourselves as best we can," said Captain Broadbeam. "If those savages should happen to come this way we'll be at their mercy."

It was almost sundown when Dave chanced to go down to the ocean front once more. He looked out to sea and then gave a cry that aroused all of the others.

"A ship! A ship!"

CHAPTER 20

AN ATTACK IN THE DARK

Dave's cry brought Captain Broadbeam to the shore in a hurry.

"Where is the ship?" he demanded.

"There!" and the young diver pointed with his hand.

"You are right, lad. But she is not headed for this island."

"Can she be the *Swallow*?"

"I should say not."

"Maybe she is the *Raven*."

"It is possible, Dave. But she is not coming here, that is certain."

"Shall we set up a shout?"

"It will do no good. They could not hear us."

"We might fly a signal of distress."

"It is too dark for that now."

Both watched the ship with interest. The captain was right, the vessel was not headed for the island, and in a few minutes it passed from view.

"If that was a friendly vessel, it's a chance gone," was Dave's sober comment.

"True, but it cannot be helped."

As usual in the tropics, night came on quickly. There was no moon, but countless stars shone from on high. The birds ceased their songs, and presently all was quiet.

"I suppose we may as well proceed to make ourselves comfortable," said Dr. Barrell.

"Somebody has got to remain on guard," came from Dave, who was not inclined to forget that the gorilla was still at large.

"We'll divide up the night into three watches of three hours each," said the captain. "I can take one watch, Dave another, and the doctor the third."

So it was arranged, and it fell to Dave to go on guard first.

"That suits me," said the young diver. "I hate to break in on my night's rest after I have once retired."

A comfortable spot had been selected for all hands. It was located about two hundred feet from the shore, where there was a series of rocks and some trees. The doctor had fashioned some brushwood into a shack, and gathered additional brushwood for bedding.

To keep himself awake Dave began to walk around the camp, and also made several trips down to the ocean front. He carried his bow and his arrows with him, to help guard against any surprise.

On his second trip down to the shore he noticed a strange fire a long distance off.

"That must be a camp-fire of some sort," he mused. "Perhaps it is that of the savages on that other island."

He watched the fire for a quarter of an hour and gradually it died away, leaving the ocean as dark as before.

It must be confessed that his day's tramping had made Dave sleepy, and it was all he could do to keep his eyes open.

"I'll be glad when it comes my turn to go to bed," he thought.

The young diver had less than half an hour to remain on guard when his attention was attracted to a peculiar sound among the trees close at hand.

He looked in the direction, and was horrified to see two shining eyes glaring down at him.

"A wild beast, sure," he reasoned. "Wonder if the thing wants to attack me?"

As quickly as he could, he got his bow into position and adjusted one of the arrows to the string.

The eyes were still turned upon him and the sight was enough to make his blood run cold.

"Here goes!" he muttered, and taking careful aim, he let the arrow fly with all force.

His aim was true, and no sooner had the arrow struck than there was an unearthly shriek, and out of the tree dropped a large dark object. It flipped and flopped over the ground, uttering snarl after snarl.

"What's the row?" cried Captain Broadbeam, leaping to his feet and seizing a club.

"I've struck something!" answered Dave. "Take care!"

"It's that gorilla!"

"So I see—now," said the young diver.

The creature was seriously but not mortally wounded and continued to flop around, uttering the most unearthly of shrieks and cries, which awoke all of the others in the camp.

"In mercy's name what does this mean?" demanded Doctor Barrell, nervously.

"Here is your gorilla, doctor!" sang out Dave. "Come and get him if you want him."

"Ugh! What a horrid creature. Is—is he dangerous still?"

"He will be if you get too close to him."

"Kill him! Kill him!" cried Bob. "Don't let him come this way!"

Watching his opportunity, Captain Broadbeam let fly with his club, hitting the gorilla in the neck. Then Dave put another arrow into the creature's body, and at last it gave a shudder and a gasp and rolled over dead.

"Kilt, is it?" came weakly from Pat Stoodles. "Sure an' it's a good job done, so it is!"

The camp-fire was stirred up and the captain picked up a torch and walked over to the gorilla.

"Dead as a stone," he announced, and then Dave and the doctor approached.

"We can save the skin and the skull," said Doctor Barrell. "They, at least, can do us no harm."

"I am glad he is dead," came from the captain. "Dave, you gave him a good one in the eye."

"I'm glad I had the bow and arrow to do it with," answered the young diver modestly.

After this Captain Broadbeam went on guard, and, utterly exhausted, Dave lay down and slept soundly until long after the sun came up on the following morning.

"Now I feel like a new man," said the young diver on arising. "I can tell you a sound sleep is a wonderful thing."

"The question is, what are we to do next?" came from the doctor. "We cannot remain on this island forever."

"Well, we shall have to remain until some ship takes us off," said Captain Broadbeam.

"And in the meantime we have got to provide for ourselves," put in Dave. "And that is not going to be so easy unless we live on clams, oysters, fish, and berries."

"Don't forget the birds," said the captain.

Dave wanted to go fishing, and after a good deal of trouble succeeded in making a hook of a big pin Bob had been using in place of a button on his jacket. For bait he used a big bug he found under a dead tree limb.

"I don't know how this is going to work," he said.

"Well, there is nothing like trying," answered the captain. "I'll see what I can do to bring down some more birds and find some fruit."

Dave started to fish in the cove, and it was not long before he got a bite and pulled in a fish weighing a couple of pounds. This encouraged him, and inside of an hour he had a mess of nine to his credit.

"We'll be able to get all the fish we want, that is sure," he reasoned. "Living on the island wouldn't be half bad, if it wasn't that those fellows on the *Raven* may sail away and get at that treasure before we have a chance to reach the spot."

Dave could not help thinking, too, of those on the *Swallow*, and he wondered how his father was faring.

Having caught all the fish he wished he was presently joined by Captain Broadbeam, who had brought down two more birds.

"I think I'll take a swim," said Dave. "I feel as if I needed the wash."

"Very well, I'll sit on the shore and watch you," replied the captain.

The young diver was soon in the water, which felt cool and refreshing. He loved to sport around, and dove and swam about to his heart's content.

"Better come in," he said to the master of the *Swallow*.

"Not today, lad," came back the answer. "How is the bottom where you are swimming?"

"Sandy, with a few shells," answered Dave. "Do you know what I am thinking?" he went on. "There may be pearls here."

"Perhaps."

"I'm going to do some diving and take a look around."

Dave was as good as his word and dove not once but a dozen times. He brought up a peck of oysters, but none containing pearls.

"Must have been mistaken," he said. "I'll try it once again."

He made a beautiful dive and reached the bottom with ease.

But scarcely had he put out his hand for an oyster when he saw something that filled him with alarm.

A long, dark object was moving along the ocean bottom towards him.

At first he could not make out what it was, but presently discovered that it was a slimy water snake. The reptile was all of ten feet in length and five or six inches in thickness.

Dave had no wish to encounter such a horrible-looking creature, and turning, he started to swim to the surface.

The water snake came after him rapidly, and just as he got his head above water Dave felt something slippery curl itself around one of his legs and start to draw him under.

CHAPTER 21

DAVE AND THE WATER SNAKE

"Help me, Captain Broadbeam!"

"What's the matter, Dave?"

"A water snake has me by the leg."

Before Dave could say more the water snake began to pull so fiercely that the head of the young diver was forced under the water.

He struggled desperately, trying his best to get away.

But now the reptile swung the fore part of its body around and embraced Dave's other leg, rendering the youth almost helpless.

The young diver kicked as hard as he could, but the reptile only clung the closer.

Down went the youth, until he felt that he must be drowned or strangled to death.

He was afraid to feel for the snake with his hands for fear of losing control of those members also.

With a wild effort he arose almost to the surface, so that he could see above him.

Whizz! It was a rope, thrown to him by Captain Broadbeam. It belonged to the rowboat and the captain had been carrying it, thinking it might be useful in one way or another.

The end of the rope just failed to reach Dave, but as soon as he saw it the young diver did his best to get hold of the object.

His breath was fast leaving him when he managed to clutch the rope with one hand. Then he drew it towards him and caught it with his other hand also.

Captain Broadbeam was watching anxiously, and as soon as he felt the rope tighten he began to haul in, slowly at first and then with might and main.

Nearer to shore came Dave, dragging the horrible water snake behind him. In vain the reptile tried to stay its progress. Then it thrashed around and caught Dave at the neck.

In self-defense the youth had to take one hand and try to force the water snake away. But this could not be done.

At last Dave could walk on the bottom, and then he struggled into shore with all speed.

As he did this, Captain Broadbeam came to his assistance, and clutched at the reptile.

But the water snake was out of its element on land, and in a trice it loosened itself, dropped back into the ocean, and disappeared.

Dave was so exhausted he pitched headlong on the sand, where he lay, panting for breath.

"Did he sting you?" queried the captain, anxiously.

"I don't think so," was the gasped-out reply. "But he came pretty close to drowning me!"

"I reckon you won't go bathing again lad."

"Not for a million dollars!"

"That's the worst of bathing in unknown waters. You don't know what you are going to run up against."

"I didn't imagine there were water snakes here."

After resting awhile, Dave dressed himself, and the pair went back to the camp.

Dave was delighted to note that Bob was recovering rapidly and that Pat Stoodles was also doing as well as could be expected.

"You want to be careful, Dave," said Bob. "We can't afford to lose you."

"And I don't want to be lost," answered the young diver, grimly.

"Have you seen anything of the savages?"

"Not a sign."

"They must wonder what has become of us."

"Perhaps they think we escaped to the ship."

"If we only had!"

"That is so, Bob, but we have got to make the best of it."

"And you can't see a sign of the ship anywhere?"

"Not the least bit of a sign."

"Too bad!" and the young engineer gave a deep sigh.

Slowly the hours dragged by. It was very warm, but there were signs of a storm in the air.

Dave set to work to gather some firewood, thinking a good fire would serve to keep them comfortable in case of a heavy rain.

"I shouldn't be surprised if we got a heavy one, when it does come," remarked Captain Broadbeam, as he gazed at the sky.

"Storms in the tropics are apt to prove severe," said Doctor Barrell.

Having collected the firewood, Dave went out with his bow and arrows to see if he could bring down some more birds.

At first he moved but a short distance from the camp, but presently he saw some extra fine birds at a distance and followed them toward the north shore of the island.

He had just brought down one bird and was trying for a second when the storm broke and the rain began to come down heavily.

"This is severe, and no mistake," he murmured. "Guess I'll have to find shelter unless I want to get soaked."

Not far away were some tall rocks, backed up by a clump of bushes and vines.

The young diver moved towards the rocks on the run. He was but a few feet away when he saw an opening in front of him—a split in the rocks of unknown depth.

He tried to step back to safety, but it was too late. His feet slipped and down he went for several yards.

"Hullo, this won't do!" he cried. "I don't want to get into another underground cave!"

He tried to climb up the rocks, but again his feet slipped and he went down a yard or two more. This time he struck a solid flooring of rocks, so to descend further was impossible.

"Thank fortune the hole isn't any deeper," he said half aloud.

The fall had shaken him up somewhat and for the minute he remained where he was, trying to get back his breath.

He noticed that the rocks around him were all perfectly smooth, but did not realize what this meant until he tried to crawl to the top of the opening.

He could not get a hold anywhere, and as often as he got up a foot or two, he slipped back again.

"Well, this is provoking, to say the least," he muttered. "How in the world am I to get out of here?"

The rain was now pouring down steadily, and in a very few minutes he was wet to the skin.

"If I had a rope or a pole I might get out," he reasoned. But he had absolutely nothing with which to help himself.

A quarter of an hour went by and then to Dave's alarm he found the water pouring into the hole steadily from a rivulet above. Soon the water was up to his ankles and it arose steadily to his knees.

The storm was now on in all of its fury, and in the forest he could hear the trees swaying and snapping under the pressure of the high wind that was blowing.

Again he made an effort to crawl out of the opening. But the rocks were now wet and slippery and afforded no foothold whatever.

The wind was increasing steadily until it blew a regular hurricane. High overhead he saw some branches of trees sailing through the air.

"I hope those in camp are safe," he said to himself.

A little later came an extra heavy blast of wind. There followed a great crashing, and in an instant a big tree fell directly over the opening, cutting off much of the light above.

One of the tree branches pressed down on Dave's head, forcing him to a sitting position in the hole.

"This is the worst yet!" he muttered, after he realized that he was not harmed. "Now I am a regular prisoner. I can't move that tree, that's sure!"

By the aid of the tree limb the young diver crawled upward until he reached the trunk across the opening.

The branches were so thick he had to literally force his way along.

The opening was almost closed by the big tree trunk, but to one side there were several loose rocks, and after an effort he succeeded in shoving them into the hole and thus making a place through which he crawled, although, not without great difficulty.

He was now free once more, and despite the fury of the elements set off for the camp with all speed.

To travel was not easy, and often he had to make a detour in order to avoid a fallen tree or a deep pool of water.

He was still a short distance from camp when there came another terrific whirl of wind that sent tree limbs flying in all directions. One struck Dave on the shoulder and hurled him flat.

"Phew! This is awful!" he muttered, and then stopped short, as a cry from a distance reached his ears.

"Help! Help!" came in Doctor Barrell's voice. "Help, or I shall be killed!"

CHAPTER 22

WHAT THE STORM BROUGHT

As quickly as he could Dave picked himself up once more and hurried into the camp.

Here he ran into Captain Broadbeam.

"Hullo, did you call?" asked the captain.

"No, it was Doctor Barrell," answered the young diver. "Where is he?"

For reply came another call from the scientific man, and now they located him down near the shore of the ocean. He was lying on his back, with a small tree pressing him down into the sand. The waves were sending their spray flying over him.

It was but the work of a moment to lift the tree. While Captain Broadbeam did this, Dave helped the doctor to crawl to a point of safety.

"Ugh! What an experience!" muttered Doctor Barrell, as he gave a shudder. "Thank you for rescuing me."

"How did it happen, doctor?" questioned Dave.

"I came out to look for you. Just as I reached the spot the wind sent the tree down and over me. I am thankful that I was not killed."

All hurried into camp, and here Dave told his story. Then they had to watch out, fearful that the storm would do them further injury.

But the wind went down as rapidly as it had come up. The rain, however, continued, and did not cease until noon of the next day.

"I don't want to encounter many such storms," said Dave, when the sun shone once more.

"You'll have to put up with them, if you remain in the tropics," answered Captain Broadbeam.

When Dave and the others went forth after the storm they picked up a great number of dead birds. The ocean shore was strewn with stranded fish.

"Here is eating enough for a month, if only it would keep," said Captain Broadbeam.

"I hope we don't have to stay here a month," answered Dave.

"Right you are, lad. But we must take what comes."

"Don't you think we'll have a spell of good weather after such a storm as this?"

"Certainly."

"Then I move we take to the boat and try to find our ship. We can take the dead birds, fish, and some oysters, clams, berries, and cocoanuts along for provisions. And also some bamboo sticks full of fresh water."

The idea appealed strongly to Captain Broadbeam and also to Doctor Barrell. Bob and the Irishman were willing to do anything that the others wished.

"Let us start out tomorrow," said the captain, and after that no time was lost in preparing for the expedition.

The rowboat was carefully overhauled, and then loaded with the things that seemed necessary to take along. Water was to be had in plenty, and they filled many big, hollow bamboo stems with it, corking up the stems until the water should be wanted.

"We must remember to keep the island in view," said the captain. "We may be glad enough to return, in case we cannot locate the *Swallow*."

At last came the time set for starting out, and Bob and Pat Stoodles were helped into the rowboat. The others followed, and the captain and Dave pushed away and took to the oars of the craft.

"I trust we find the ship," sighed Bob. In his weakened condition he longed for the comforts which had been denied to him while on the island.

"So do I hope we find the *Swallow*," answered Dave.

"We must keep a close watch for those savages," came from Captain Broadbeam. "I shouldn't wish to fall into their hands again."

"Bad cess to thim!" cried Pat Stoodles. "Niver do I want to set me eyes on thim ag'in!"

The rowboat passed around one corner of the island and all looked eagerly for some sign of a sail.

"Nothing in sight," said Dave.

"I see something drifting upon the waves," announced the doctor.

All looked in the direction which he pointed out and saw a large mass of driftwood floating toward them.

"That means a wreck of some sort," cried the captain. "Let us make an investigation."

The others were willing, and not long after this they came up beside the wreckage, which proved to be a spar with cordage and part of a forecastle and rail.

"Can that wreckage be from the *Swallow*?" asked Dave, anxiously.

"It may be," answered the captain. "Still, I am not sure."

"Perhaps it is from the *Raven*," came from Doctor Barrell.

"I'd rather it was from that vessel than from our own," said the young diver, quickly. "But it may be from the *Swallow*, and I'll tell you why," he added, suddenly.

"Well?"

"Don't you remember about Pete Rackley? He may have disabled our ship."

"If he has done so he should be swung from a yardarm," came from Captain Broadbeam, hotly.

As they could make nothing of the wreckage they allowed it to drift by and continued their journey around another point of the island.

Not to tire themselves, they took turns at rowing.

Bob and Stoodles were made as comfortable as possible on the seats, with palm branches laid over them, to protect them from the fierce rays of the sun.

Thus an hour passed and still nothing of importance came to view.

They saw some more wreckage at a distance, and rowing up to it, discovered several empty chicken crates and an empty water cask.

"These prove nothing," said the captain. "The crates may have been thrown overboard on purpose."

"It's strange, with so much wreckage around, we don't sight some ship," said Dave.

"You are right, lad, for that wreckage is not water-soaked and old."

Before long they began to grow hungry, and stopped their search long enough to get a lunch of berries and cold fish, washed down with water from one of the bamboo stems.

"This is a great way to carry water," was Dave's comment. "It keeps it very sweet."

"So it does, Dave," said the doctor. "But the water is bound to evaporate very rapidly."

The lunch over, they resumed their journey. They had put far out to sea on one side of the island. Now they returned, to put out on the opposite side.

They were within three hundred feet of the island when Doctor Barrell set up a cry of warning.

"Stop! Do not land!"

"What's the matter, doctor?" came from the captain. "We were not going to land. We are bound for the other side of the island."

"I saw some persons moving behind yonder bushes and rocks," went on the man of science.

"Saw somebody?" said Dave.

"Yes."

"White men?"

"No, savages!"

"Are you sure of this?" demanded Captain Broadbeam.

"I—I think I am," stammered the doctor.

"Where are they?"

"Gone now."

"Perhaps you were mistaken, doctor," said Dave.

"It is possible—but I do not think so."

The rowboat was allowed to drift, and all gazed earnestly toward the island. But not a person of any sort appeared.

"This is mighty strange," was the captain's comment. "The savages couldn't have been there when we left."

"Maybe they just arrived," said Dave.

"That is possible. Still—"

"I—I may have been mistaken," said Doctor Barrell. "Remember, my eyesight is not of the best."

"I wish we were sure of this," went on the captain. "If the savages are on the island in force I don't know as we shall care to go back, even if we don't locate the ship."

"Perhaps they are hiding, thinking that we will return," said Dave. "One thing is sure, we have got to be careful of what we do after this."

They talked the matter over for a few minutes more and then resumed their journey to the other side of the island. They kept their eyes toward the shore, but neither man nor beast came to view.

"Maybe he saw some gorillas," said Bob, who had listened to the talk. "They look like savages from a distance."

"Well, a lot of gorillas would be as bad as a band of savages," answered Dave.

Slowly the rowboat proceeded on its journey until they rounded another point of the island. Then Dave set up a shout of dismay.

"What is it?" questioned the captain and the doctor quickly.

"Savages! They are after us in their canoes!"

The young diver spoke the truth. There, at no great distance from the island shore, were two long war canoes, each filled with the enemy.

As soon as the savages discovered the whites they set up a mad yell of delight, and then hurried in pursuit of our friends.

CHAPTER 23

ON THE SHIP ONCE MORE

"We are in for it now!" cried Dave, as he watched the approach of the two war canoes loaded down with savages.

"It certainly looks like it," muttered Captain Broadbeam, grimly. "Well, a man can die but once, and we had better fight to the bitter end."

"That is true," came from Doctor Barrell. "But I am afraid that three against two dozen or more will make a poor showing."

The savages now became aware that they were discovered, and they set up a fierce shout. Those at the long sweeps began to row more swiftly than ever, as if thirsting for the blood of the whites.

"If we only had a gun or two," said Dave. "But we haven't a thing."

"Only the oars, and they'll make poor weapons," answered Captain Broadbeam. "I'm afraid it's all up with us, lad. We must look for the worst."

"Can't we outdistance them by rowing?"

"I think not."

"But we might reach shore again and take to the jungle. That will be better than being slaughtered on the ocean."

"Yes, yes, let us try for the shore!" burst out the doctor. "We have at least a fighting chance of reaching it."

As quickly as possible the rowboat was turned about, and its bow pointed to a distant headland. All pulled with might and main, the perspiration pouring down their faces and backs.

But it was useless. The war canoes crept closer and closer.

And now, as if to make doubly sure of them, there suddenly appeared upon the beach another crowd of natives, brandishing knives and war clubs.

The din was hideous, and the cry from the shore was echoed and re-echoed by the savages in the canoes.

They felt certain that the whites would become their prisoners.

Captain, doctor, and young diver looked at each other with blanched faces.

They felt that their last hour on earth was at hand.

Swiftly the war canoes came closer.

Then of a sudden something happened which came as a great shock to our friends and as an even greater shock to the savages.

Boom!

Dull and sullen a ship's gun boomed out and a shot sped across the bow of the foremost of the canoes.

"A shot!" said Captain Broadbeam, leaping to his feet. "What can it mean?"

"It means that there is a steamship in sight!" cried Dave. "See the smoke around the bend of the island. Here she comes!"

"It is the *Swallow*!" came from the doctor. "Heaven be praised!"

The physician was right; it was indeed the *Swallow*, and now another shot boomed out.

The ball struck the stern of the leading war canoe, and the craft began immediately to fill with water.

The yelling was terrific, for the natives were taken completely by surprise.

As the first of the canoes began to sink, those on board leaped into the water.

Some started for the other canoe, but the majority swam toward shore, thinking that the second craft would soon be served like the first.

But the natives on the shore were not yet daunted, and with another yell they let fly a shower of arrows at those in the rowboat.

"Down!" cried Captain Broadbeam, and all hurled themselves to the bottom of the craft.

It was well that they did this, for the arrows must otherwise have killed one or more of them.

Boom! A third shot from the *Swallow* was now directed at those on shore.

The aim was a good one and two natives were seen to pitch forward, to rise no more.

Seeing this, the others took to their heels with all speed and disappeared into the jungle.

It was the last of the attack upon our friends.

The savages had had enough of the contest and now thought only of saving themselves.

The second canoe was beached in a great hurry and the occupants disappeared as if by magic.

As soon as they felt free to do so, our friends resumed their oars and rowed in the direction of the *Swallow*.

On the deck they saw the lieutenant of the ship, Amos Fearless, and several other familiar faces.

Soon the steamship and the rowboat came together, and then Bob and Pat Stoodles were hoisted aboard the larger craft. Dave, the captain, and the doctor followed.

"Father!" cried Dave, and rushed into his parent's arms.

Amos Fearless could not speak, but his face showed plainly his great joy.

"And how are you, father?" went on his son.

"He is doing nicely," answered the first mate of the *Swallow*. "But his speech has not yet come back to him."

Bob and Pat Stoodles were carried to state-rooms, and here Doctor Barrell proceeded to minister to their comforts through the stock in his medicine chest.

While this was going on Captain Broadbeam started in to learn if Pete Rackley had shown himself.

"Why, certainly; he is on board," said the mate. "He's a poor, down-hearted castaway, isn't he?"

"He's a rascal!" burst out Captain Broadbeam. "Where is he? I'll put him in irons!"

A search was at once instituted and at last Pete Rackley was found hiding in the forecastle.

He was the picture of misery when brought before Captain Broadbeam.

"It's all a mistake," he said, in a trembling voice. "All a mistake."

"It is no mistake," said the captain, sternly. "Dave Fearless is here to testify against you."

"But—but—"

"You need make no more denials, Rackley. You have played the game and lost. Now answer me truthfully: Have you done any harm as yet to the *Swallow*?"

"No! No!"

"You are telling the truth?"

"I am—I swear it."

"I will order a strict investigation. If anything is wrong—"

And the captain ended with a stern shake of his forefinger at the rascal.

Pete Rackley was then bound and cast into the brig of the ship.

The assistant engineer was closely questioned, and he said Rackley had been seen frequently around the engine room.

Then the entire machinery of the ship was inspected.

At one point several bolts were found filed almost in two.

At another point an oil cup was broken, so that the part might get dry and thus cause considerable delay.

These things were all mended, and Captain Broadbeam ordered that Rackley be chained up in the brig because of his falsehoods.

The day was spent in the vicinity of the island, looking for the *Raven*, but that vessel failed to appear.

By the next morning both Bob and Pat Stoodles were pronounced out of danger by the doctor.

A conference was held and it was decided that the *Swallow* should now proceed with all haste to the spot where the *Happy Hour* had gone down with the treasure.

Nothing of special interest happened for several days.

Bob Vilett grew better rapidly and was able to be around at the end of a week.

Pat Stoodles' recovery was slower. But to the satisfaction of the friends he had made it was seen that the Irish castaway's mind was becoming clearer every day.

"He'll be as clear-headed as any of us when he gets on his feet once more," said Doctor Barrell, and his statement proved correct.

Day after day went by and the *Swallow* kept steadily to her course.

Amos Fearless was now as well as ever excepting for his voice.

He could occasionally speak a few words in a hoarse whisper, but that was all; and he would sometimes break down in the midst of a sentence.

This grieved Dave very much, but he could do nothing for the sufferer.

"It is time alone can do it," said Doctor Barrell, encouragingly.

But Dave was downcast. What if his father should never be able to talk again as of old?

"I'd rather let the fortune go than have that happen," he told himself, over and over again. He was afraid that the affliction might grow worse, so that his parent would not be able to make any sound at all!

CHAPTER 24

ATTACKED BY A FIRE FISH

"And this is the spot where the *Happy Hour* went down?"

"It is, according to the markings on the chart, Dave."

"And how deep do you reckon the ocean is at this point?"

"The chart says 12,500 feet—a little over two miles."

"It is a deep distance. Regular divers could never make it. They would be crushed to death by the mere pressure of the water."

"I have thought the matter over, Dave, and I think it will be best for both you and your father to go down only a half-mile the first day. Then, if that is successful, you can go a little deeper each day, until the bottom is reached. And you will have to use the diving bell at all times."

"I know that. And if we leave the diving bell at all it will have to be in those new steel-ribbed diving suits we had made in Washington especially for this trip," concluded the young diver.

The *Swallow* lay at rest on the broad bosom of the mighty Pacific Ocean.

Nothing had been seen of the *Raven*, and at present not a sign of a strange sail showed itself anywhere.

It was high noon, and Captain Broadbeam had just concluded his calculations to prove that he was at the very spot which was said to be that where the *Happy Hour* had sunk.

Dave looked thoughtfully over the side, into the greenish waves, lit for a depth of only thirty or forty feet below the surface.

What fortune did that silent body of water hold for his father and himself?

A touch on his elbow aroused him, and turning, he found his parent standing beside him.

Amos Fearless could not say a word, but he motioned to the water and smiled. Then he spoke to Dave in the sign language of the divers.

"This is the spot," he signed. "How soon does Captain Broadbeam calculate to let us go down?"

"I think tomorrow," replied Dave.

A long talk followed, by word of mouth on Dave's part and by signs on the part of the parent.

It was a sad sight to see Amos Fearless try to talk with his mouth and fail. His tongue would cling to his teeth and refuse to budge. At last he turned away with tears in his eyes and Dave was equally affected.

The remainder of the day was spent in getting the diving bell into shape for use.

This was inspected with great care, for it was understood by all that the two divers, father and son, would be taking their lives in their hands in going down such an immense distance as contemplated.

"It's strange we don't see anything of the *Raven*," said Dave to Captain Broadbeam.

"Perhaps Lemuel Hankers knows enough to keep out of our reach," was the answer. "He may know that we—or rather, you—are on board and have exposed Pete Rackley, and he may wish to keep his own head out of danger."

"That must be it."

"If Hankers came near us I would be apt to make it hot for him."

"And I'll do the same."

It was a clear day overhead when Dave and his father entered the diving bell and were hoisted over the side of the *Swallow*.

Slowly the immense cable unwound itself, letting the bell down deeper and deeper.

Soon the light of day was shut out and all became as black as night and as cold as a tomb.

Amos Fearless turned on the electric current and the diving bell sent out several rays of light.

The light attracted numerous fish, who swam up swiftly, only to stop just as fast and gaze stupidly through the glass of the bell's sides.

There was one fish in particular, commonly called the electric-light fish, the scientific name being linophyrne lucifer, which had what looked like an electric light on the end of its sharp snout and a rope-like appendage under its lower jaw. It had a square mouth and sharp, curved teeth, and a look which was enough to give an ordinary mortal a chill.

"We must secure a specimen of that fish," said Amos Fearless, in the sign language. "The captain and the doctor spoke about it particularly."

"And also a specimen of that long, thin thing," answered Dave, pointing to what is familiarly called in Borneo the ray of fire. The ray of fire is a white fish four or five feet long and less than three inches thick. It has silver scales which flash out like fire whenever it swims quickly.

Soon they had reached the half-mile limit, and the diving bell came to a standstill.

Then a door in the bell was opened and they prepared to spread out a strong net with which to catch what was desired.

It was by no means an easy task—indeed, the most of a diver's labors are very hard, and before the net was properly adjusted both Dave and his parent were almost winded.

Then they moved the diving bell around, from one spot to another, on the lookout for the electric-light fish and the ray of fire, so called.

Soon they saw one of the electric-light fish in the vicinity.

They had brought some bait along, and this was tied up in the net.

The monstrous fish scented the bait and came forward slowly and cautiously.

He was hungry, yet he did not altogether like the appearance of the diving bell.

He had never seen a live human being before, although he had feasted upon the body of more than one dead sailor, coming down with some wreck.

Amos Fearless and Dave remained as motionless as statues.

Nearer and nearer came the electric-light fish.

The light on his snout blinked and winked in an odd fashion and was once or twice turned upon Dave and his father.

Then, like a flash, the monstrous fish swept into the net after the bait.

Snap! went the line attached to the top of the net, and Dave and his father began pulling the net shut with might and main.

They had to work like lightning, for, feeling that something was wrong, the electric-light fish began to thrash around at a lively rate.

The net swept to and fro as the fish darted hither and thither in its efforts to escape.

Bang!

Up against the diving bell came net and fish with a shock that threatened to shiver the glass into a million fragments.

"Shove away!" motioned Amos Fearless to his son, and Dave caught hold of a rod to which the net was fastened and the net was placed at a distance from the bell.

At last the wonderful electric-light fish was a prisoner in the net. It still continued to thrash around, and fearful that he might break loose in spite of the strength of the net, Amos Fearless signaled to those on the ship to haul up the prize.

Slowly the net ascended until it was out of sight and only the occasional blinking of the fish's light lit up the path he was taking to the outside world. Then even this died out.

"A good haul," said Amos Fearless, in the sign language. "Now for that ray of fire and our day's work will be done. And I will be glad of it."

"So will I be glad," answered Dave. "We'll want several days down here in order to get used to deep-sea work once more."

The diving bell was supplied with a second net—smaller and of a much tighter mesh, and this they now put out in the hope of catching one of the rays of fire.

Two were in the vicinity and eying the bell and those inside with much curiosity.

"Nasty, snaky-looking things," observed Dave, as he helped to bait the net. "And they look wicked, too."

"All of the deep-sea fish are wicked-looking," was the answer. "I never saw anything different."

They waited for fully ten minutes before one of the strange fishes came up to the net.

Then it darted inside and began biting at the bait.

"We've got him!" cried Dave, and began to pull on the string which shut the net up.

At once the ray of fire tried to escape.

But it was too late, for the top of the net closed tight just as he shoved his nose against it.

Then an odd thing happened.

The fish began to lash around in a circle, emitting a strange sound like the roll of distant thunder.

Sparks flew from its tail which dropped down into the water like the sparks from a Roman candle.

"What a beautiful sight!" began Dave, when of a sudden he heard a swishing through the water.

He turned, to behold his father in a truly perilous situation.

The second ray of fire had come up and wound itself around Amos Fearless' neck.

Its hard body was like a wand of rubber, and unless the fish were released the old diver would speedily be strangled to death!

CHAPTER 25

LEFT TO PERISH

For one moment Dave Fearless' heart seemed to stop beating.

The sight before him was a terrible one.

Vainly was his father struggling to free himself from the deadly embrace of the creature which had attacked him.

There were three coils of the ray of fire around the old diver's neck and these were slowly but surely choking the life out of the man.

His eyes were bulging from their sockets—his tongue stuck from his mouth. In a few seconds more all would be over.

Close at hand stuck a knife in a case on the wall of the diving bell.

With a leap Dave secured the blade. Another leap and he was at his parent's side.

But how should he attack the strange, snake-like fish? A false cut and he might stab his father in the throat.

But he must act, or it would be too late.

With a cautious movement of the knife he slit the fish along the back.

There was a strange hissing and the ray of fire swung loose the end of its tail.

It caught Dave around the wrist, holding that member as in a vise.

At first the youth was inclined to drop the knife, but he managed to hold on.

Then began an intensely interesting struggle between boy and fish.

Dave tried his best to twist the hand around so that he might cut the fish a second time.

He brought up his other hand, in an endeavor to transfer the knife, but as quick as a flash the ray of fire unloosened itself and caught both wrists.

In its own way it was fighting for its mate, a prisoner in the net.

Dave's two hands were now drawn tightly to his father's throat, as if the horrible monster of the deep meant to make the boy strangle his own parent!

"I must get my hand free!" thought the young diver.

Again he struggled, the sweat standing out on his forehead inside of his diving helmet.

At last he managed to turn one wrist and got the point of the knife again into the fish's body.

He cut and twisted as best he could and felt the ray of fire quiver with pain and rage.

The fish could not stand the cutting and presently raised its head in order to make a new move.

Exerting all of his strength, Dave made a slash at the head and cut into the light on the fish's snout.

A rush of phosphorescent blood followed, and on the instant all of the light died out in the creature's body.

Again Dave made a cut, striking deep into the fish, so deeply in fact that he made an ugly scratch on his father's neck.

This last blow was too much for the ray of fire, and slowly it fell away and floated off, Dave did not know to where.

Freed from his captor, Amos Fearless sank in a heap at the door of the diving bell.

Was he dead?

In frantic haste the youth pulled himself and his parent into the bell and shut the door.

Then he gave a quick signal to be raised to the surface.

There was no immediate answer, and a fresh alarm took possession of the young diver.

"What does this mean? Why don't they pull us up?" he asked himself.

Generally the life-line, as it is termed, is watched constantly, and every signal of a diver is acted upon on the instant.

Were this not so, many a man of the deep would go down never to come up.

A minute went by and still the signal remained unanswered.

To the boy the time seemed an age.

Feeling that his parent might die before being brought up, he began to empty the diving bell of water.

There was a fresh-air hose attached to the bell, and as the water was forced out the air came in, until at last the bell was as dry as a hogshead that has been emptied.

The moment the water was out, Dave began to work upon his diving suit.

It was no easy job to get it off without assistance.

Generally one diver helped the other, but he could obtain no aid from that form now lying stiff and motionless upon the floor of the diving bell.

At last his arms and his head were free and he turned his attention to his parent.

He unscrewed the helmet and then the rest of the old diver's suit.

Amos Fearless was almost black in the face and there was an ugly mark around his throat, mingling with the blood from the scratch Dave had caused.

Putting his ear to his parent's breast, the boy made out that his father still breathed faintly.

In the diving bell was some liquor, to be used for restorative purposes, and some of this Dave poured down his father's throat.

But still the man did not stir, and Dave began to rub his hands and move his arms, that his lungs might again get into working order.

Ten minutes passed and at last Amos Fearless gave a slight gasp.

Taking this for a good sign, Dave continued his labors and was presently rewarded by seeing his father open his eyes and shudder.

"Father! Are you all right now?" asked the boy.

The only reply was a groan. But then Amos Fearless gave a long breath, and Dave knew that he was saved.

"You had a narrow escape, father," he said. "The light fish tried to strangle you. I had to cut him to pieces with the knife. I cut you a little on the neck, but that couldn't be helped."

Amos Fearless made a feeble sign. "I know—brave boy," was what he said, and caught his son by the hand.

In the meantime the ray of fire in the net was still threshing around on the outside of the bell.

But to this fish they now paid no attention.

"Let us go up," signed Mr. Fearless, after a pause of a few minutes.

"I have signaled," was the son's answer.

"I will signal again."

He pulled the cord several times in lively fashion.

Then he waited—five seconds—ten seconds—a full minute. And still the diving bell did not move.

"They have given up watching the life-line," he reasoned. "How careless! I'll give Captain Broadbeam a talking to when they do haul us up."

"Something must be wrong," said the father, in his sign language. "Captain Broadbeam would not forget us in this fashion."

Slowly the minutes went by and each instant father and son grew more anxious.

They could not ascend of themselves, nor could they leave the diving bell and float to the surface.

Had they left the bell without their suits the water would have crushed them, for the pressure was enormous at this distance under the surface.

The air in the diving bell was anything but pure, and now of a sudden it stopped coming in altogether.

"We are lost!" cried Dave. "We shall be smothered to death!"

"I cannot believe Captain Broadbeam has forgotten us," signed Amos Fearless. "As I said before, something must be wrong!"

The old diver was right; something was very wrong on board of the *Swallow*.

While the two divers were at work under the surface of the ocean, a wild cry had arisen on board of the ship, a cry which thrilled everyone who heard it to the heart.

It came from the cook's galley and was quickly taken up on all sides.

"Fire! Fire! The ship is on fire!"

The report was true. Some fat on the cook's stove had boiled over and taken fire, and now the burning fat was flowing in all directions.

It looked as if the *Swallow* and all on board of her were doomed!

CHAPTER 26

THE BATTLE OF THE FISHES

"Fire! Fire! Fire!"

This cry, echoing throughout the *Swallow*, is the most dreadful that sailors on the high seas know.

What hope is there for those on board of a ship going down in mid-ocean, thousands of miles from land?

"We must put out that fire!" came from Captain Broadbeam. "Man the fire hose and send word to the engine room to turn on the water!"

His orders were obeyed as quickly as possible.

Yet everything takes time, and before the hose could be brought into play the cook's galley was a mass of flames from beginning to end.

The wind was blowing the sparks directly forward, so the captain had the ship swung round, that the fire might be carried largely over the side.

A bucket corps was formed and they, too, poured all the water possible on the conflagration.

It was fierce, hot work, and for some time it looked as if the fire would get the best of the workers and destroy the *Swallow*.

Small wonder then that Amos Fearless and Dave were for the time being forgotten.

Ten minutes went by—twenty minutes—and both began to grow desperate.

"We must perish!" groaned Dave.

Amos Fearless shook his head, dismally.

Both became too weak to stand up, and sank on the floor of the diving bell.

The air was now stale and made them sleepy.

Gradually Dave's eyes closed.

He tried to arouse himself, but the effort was a failure.

It was the beginning of the sleep of death, and the young diver knew it!

He caught his father's hand and a warm grasp was exchanged in silence.

After that all became as a dream to the young diver.

He thought he was out in the ocean and that numerous fierce fish were swimming close to him.

Then one large fish swallowed him and he found himself cut off from all air.

He fought desperately and at last cut a hole in the fish's side and stepped out into the upper world.

Oh, how good the fresh air tasted. He filled his lungs and took breath after breath—and then—

Dave opened his eyes and stared vacantly around him. He was on the deck of the *Swallow* and Doctor Barrell was bending over him, a look of deep anxiety on the kindly face.

"Dave, how do you feel now?" came in anxious tones. "Can you breathe?"

He could not answer excepting to take a long breath; but he now understood the situation. He had been hauled up to the *Swallow's* deck and was saved! Then of a sudden he became unconscious again.

Quarter of an hour later Dave found himself sitting up and swallowing some medicine Doctor Barrell was forcing into his mouth. He still felt very weak, and when he tried to stand, all swam before his eyes.

"You must keep quiet, lad," said the doctor. "You have had a narrow escape from death."

"My father—" began Dave. He could say no more.

"He was brought up with you, of course."

"And is he—is he—"

"He is slowly recovering, but of course he is older than you and not so strong, and it will, consequently, take longer."

"But he will get well?"

"I think so."

After that Dave was silent for a long while. Then Captain Broadbeam came in, his face covered with smoke and grime.

"I suppose you thought we had deserted you," said the captain. "We had a hot time of it, I can tell you."

"A hot time? What do you mean?"

"Don't you know the ship has been afire, lad?"

"No."

"Well, it has been, and that's why we didn't haul you up before. I was afraid we were all bound for Davy Jones' locker, sure."

Of course, Dave was surprised and he listened to the particulars of the fire with interest.

"The galley is burned off clean and clear," said the captain, "and we've got an ugly hole in the forward deck. But otherwise the ship is all right."

The remainder of the day was spent in cleaning up the muss, and then the ship's carpenter went to work, with several sailor assistants, to build a new galley and mend the burned deck.

It was several days before Dave felt able to do any more diving, and even then it was only the thought of locating the sunken treasure that made him go down.

Amos Fearless was too weak to do anything, so Dave had to go down alone.

"Be sure and pull me up," said the young diver, as he was about to enter the diving bell.

"I will see to that," replied Amos Fearless, in his sign language. "Don't stay down too long."

Down and down into the dark and cold waters of the Pacific sank the diving bell.

The trip before had been about half a mile; this time Dave intended to go down twice that distance.

If this trip was successful he was resolved, on the next day, weather permitting, to go down to the very bottom, two miles below the surface.

After what seemed a journey without end the diving bell came to a stop.

The mile limit had been reached.

The young diver turned on the electric lights and gazed around him, curiously.

He gave a start of surprise, and not without reason.

The waters were no longer dark and black.

There was a peculiar glow of light coming up from somewhere below, and in the water floated something closely resembling smoke or clouds.

"What did this mean?"

"It's like another world," he thought. "And what strange fish!"

But then he caught sight of something which filled him with alarm.

A number of small fish had come up around the diving bell and were now swarming all over it, inside and out.

Each fish was less than six inches long, but there were hundreds of them darting hither and thither, churning up the water as before, and emitting a strange, hissing sound.

He tried to get back to the diving bell, but found the effort a failure.

The fish swam against him, plunging and leaping, and finally turned him completely over.

He was in the power of a new enemy, and what the end of this adventure would be there was no telling.

The fish were indeed curious—some long and thin, others short and fat, but all with something extremely unusual in their make-up.

One fish had horns on its head, another had wings like those of a bird, and many had feathers instead of scales on their bodies.

And then came a fish shaped very much like a long, spiral spring, with a square-looking head and horns all of two feet long just over his eyes, which set out like two yellow and white eggs.

"I must try and get you, my beauty," thought the young diver, and prepared to put out the net for that purpose.

He had to work with care, being alone, and it took considerable time before he opened the diving bell and let in the water.

The first thing that struck him when he felt the water on him was that it was no longer cold, but warm—even warmer than at the surface.

This was not unpleasant, but he could not help but wonder how much hotter it might be at the very bottom.

"This part of the ocean may be over a submarine volcano," he reasoned. "If that is so it will be boiling at the bottom, and to get to the wreck will be impossible."

At last his net was set and he baited it with care.

Then he waited.

Several small fish came up and nibbled at his bait, but not the spiral fish he was after.

"He's a shy one," thought Dave. "He's not going to be caught if he knows it."

But at last the young diver was rewarded by seeing two of the spiral fish approaching.

One apparently urged the other on, until both came into the net and began to chew at the bait, which was purposely very tough.

With all speed Dave set to work to shut the net.

This was no easy task for a single person, and in order to accomplish it the young diver had to step outside of the diving bell.

He was just finishing up the task when a strange rushing behind him caused him to turn around.

At first he could see but little, for the water behind him was churned up into a milk-white foam. Then he saw a great mass of little fishes pressing toward him.

CHAPTER 27

THE RIVAL DIVERS

"Gosh, but this is something new!"

So thought Dave Fearless as he tried to pass the little fish in order to get into the diving bell.

But the little chaps were both frisky and powerful and got in his way continually.

They smelt of his legs, his body and his head, and then each gave him a resounding slap with the tail.

It was like a hundred tack hammers playing a tattoo over his entire body.

Never had the young diver been in such a peculiar position before.

At last he hit out straight ahead of him.

It was like striking into a mass of jelly.

The little fish flew in all directions, only to return the moment the young diver's arm was hauled back.

Slowly but surely, however, he got closer to the diving bell.

At last he gained the door and hauled himself inside by main strength.

The bell was full of the tiny fish, and he had literally to squeeze them out in order to squeeze himself in.

Once in the bell he hardly knew what to do next.

To shut the door under the circumstances was out of the question.

Yet he could not remain below the surface forever.

But while he was meditating upon the unexpected turn of affairs some other fish came to his aid.

They were long, fat fellows, with stomachs on them resembling balloons.

There were a score or more of them, and they began to gobble down the little fish as rapidly as they could swallow them.

A fight ensued between the little fish and the big fish, and in the end nearly all of the fish of both sorts left the vicinity of the diving bell for parts unknown.

Realizing what was going on, Dave watched his chance and when only a few of each kind of fish remained in the diving bell he shut the door.

Then he began to pump out the water, and at the same time signaled to those on the ship to raise him to the surface.

"A splendid haul!" cried Doctor Barrell, on examining his strange catch. "Two spiral whipsnaps, to use the vulgar name, and half a dozen fish which are new to science."

Captain Broadbeam had taken up one of the little fish and was examining it with interest.

The fish was dead, having been cut open during the struggle in the diving bell.

"He's got something inside of him that don't belong there, I reckon," said the captain. "Creation, look here!"

And he held up—a small gold coin!

"A gold coin!" cried Dave. "A Chinese piece, too!"

"You are right," said Doctor Barrell.

"Perhaps it came from the sunken treasure," put in Amos Fearless, who stood near.

"Perhaps."

"Then the treasure must be down here, at the bottom of the ocean," added Dave.

"It's not unlikely," said the doctor. "Although such a fish might swim a long distance with such a coin in his insides."

While the party was talking the matter over, and Doctor Barrell was preparing to place the spiral fish in a safe place, there came a cry from the lookout:

"Sail oh!"

"Where away?" cried Captain Broadbeam.

"Dead ahead, sir."

"Can you make her out?"

"A steamer, sir."

"Perhaps it is the *Raven*," said Dave. And his heart gave a leap.

Slowly the newcomer came closer until, at noon, she was within hailing distance.

She was really the *Raven* and she came up boldly, with Lemuel Hankers, Bart, and several others on her deck.

The *Raven* would have gained the spot several days before, but an unexpected breakdown of her machinery had caused a delay.

The wait was maddening to Lemuel Hankers and his son, yet their rage did them no good.

The *Raven* came to a standstill when within hailing distance of the *Swallow*.

"*Raven*, ahoy!" shouted Captain Broadbeam, through his speaking trumpet.

"Ahoy, the *Swallow*!" came back from Captain Nesik.

"You're a pretty set of rascals!" burst out the honest commander of the Government vessel.

"Don't talk that way to us!" retorted Captain Nesik.

"Why didn't you rescue us from the savages?"

"We were running on a reef and had to look after our ship," was the lame excuse.

"You're a set of rascals!" burst out Dave Fearless, and he shook his fist at those on the *Raven*.

"Don't call me a rascal!" said Lemuel Hankers.

"But you are one, and your son is another," came from Dave. "The mask is off, and in the future you had better keep your distance, or there will be trouble for you."

"What are you doing here?" demanded Bart, leaning on the rail.

"You know well enough."

"You are after the sunken treasure."

"If we are it is because it belongs to my father and myself," retorted Dave.

"We are on the high seas," came from Lemuel Hankers. "The treasure was abandoned, and it will belong to whoever succeeds in raising it—if it can be raised."

"By gum! I reckon he's right there," muttered Captain Broadbeam.

"Well, we intend to raise it, so you had better clear out," said Dave, boldly.

At this there arose a howl of derision from those on the *Raven*.

"Go ahead and do as you please," came from Lemuel Hankers. "But let me tell you, you have got to have pretty slick divers to get ahead of those I have hired."

"Whom have you?" questioned Captain Broadbeam, curiously.

"I am not afraid to let you know—Cal Vixen and Sam Walton."

At this announcement the faces of Captain Broadbeam, Amos Fearless, and Dave fell.

Cal Vixen and Sam Walton were known to be the best divers on the Pacific coast.

What Amos Fearless and his son had done on the Atlantic shore for the Government, Cal Vixen and Sam Walton had accomplished on the Pacific shore.

"Rivals for fair!" murmured Dave.

"Yes, my lad," answered Captain Broadbeam. "I reckon it will be nip an' tuck between ye!" And he shook his head doubtfully.

There was a pause in the talk.

"Have you a castaway on board?" questioned Lemuel Hankers, at length.

"No, but we've got a prisoner named Pete Rackley," answered Captain Broadbeam, with a chuckle.

"A prisoner!"

"Exactly—and you know what for, Lemuel Hankers, you old fraud!" said Dave.

"I? I know nothing."

"You know everything. Your well-laid plot failed to work, and Pete Rackley shall remain a prisoner until we can hand him over to the United States authorities."

A wordy quarrel followed, and presently the two rival divers came forward.

"We are going down tomorrow," said Vixen, the leader of the pair. "If you go down, mind and keep your distance."

"You mind and keep yours!" retorted Dave. "Remember, neither I nor my father can be scared by you."

"We have been hired to bring up that treasure and we mean to do it."

"I expect to do the same thing—and you shall not stop me."

"All right. Only look out, or you'll be running up a lot of trouble on your back!" came from Vixen, and then he and his mate fell back, and the two ships drifted apart, out of talking distance.

"They mean business," said Dave, to Captain Broadbeam.

"Yes, and they will cause you a lot of trouble if they can," replied the captain. "Watch them closely, every time they come near you."

The next day the hunt for the sunken treasure began in earnest.

CHAPTER 28

THE DEMONS OF THE DEEP

As early in the day as possible Captain Broadbeam made another astronomical calculation and worked out the position of the *Swallow* on his set of charts.

It was found that the ship lay about one hundred yards to the westward of where the *Happy Hour* was reported to have gone down.

This was not much, but the captain immediately gave orders that the ship be brought to the correct position.

"You'll have work enough locating her as it is," said the captain. "More than likely the ocean current has shifted her considerably."

Luckily Amos Fearless was now feeling much better, having quite recovered from his experience at the time of the fire on the ship.

With the *Raven* on the scene, it was decided by father and son that the diving bell should be taken directly to the ocean's bottom, if the thing could be accomplished.

"I know we are running a risk," said the old diver, in his sign language, "but we must be the first to discover the *Happy Hour*, no matter what the cost. To suffer defeat would kill me."

By ten o'clock in the morning the diving bell was over the side and father and son had entered it.

Those on the *Raven* were also getting out a diving bell, and Vixen and Walton were busy overhauling their deep-sea outfits.

It was indeed to be a race for the treasure.

Soon Dave and his parent had left the outside world behind and were going down and down into the mighty ocean's depths.

On this occasion it had been agreed not to look for anything but the sunken treasure ship; consequently, the fish net and several other similar appliances had been left behind.

In their places the diving bell contained several tools for digging and hauling and also several under-water firearms, for use against a possible enemy. In addition to the firearms, father and son had provided themselves with long and sharp knives.

"There is no telling what we may run across away down there," said Amos Fearless, in his sign language. "We are taking our lives in our hands, to my way of thinking."

And what he said was true—as events speedily proved.

Soon they passed through the darker portion of the ocean and knew that the first mile of the downward journey had been covered.

Then those above lowered more slowly and watched keenly for the first signal that danger might be encountered by those below.

"See, it is growing lighter," said Dave, presently, and turned off the electric lights.

His father had his hand upon the glass side of the diving bell.

"It is also growing warmer," motioned the parent, in his sign language.

A mile and a half had been covered and now the waters of the ocean were so clear and light that they could see for a hundred feet about them.

The water glistened and sparkled like diamonds as it washed against the sides of the diving bell.

"The light is growing brighter," observed Dave, presently. "Isn't it wonderful!"

They now felt they were approaching the bottom of the Pacific, for the diving bell was moving very slowly. Soon they saw great, ribbon-like grasses, the ends floating upward past the diving bell.

At this Amos Fearless shook his head.

"We don't want to get caught in those grasses," he signed. "They may prove worse than ropes of wire."

Suddenly a slight jar on the bottom of the diving bell told them that the machine had struck something. It no longer descended, but wabbled from side to side.

At once Amos Fearless signaled through the air-tube to stop lowering. Then a small glass trap was opened in the diving bell's bottom.

Through this they saw what had caused the machine to stop. It was caught in the top-most branches of a submarine tree. Below them, upon all sides, was a regular submarine forest.

The trees were two to three hundred feet tall, twisted and gnarled in all directions, with branches stretching out of their sight.

Some of the trees boasted of most gorgeous flowers, while from others floated what looked like luscious fruits.

Below the trees could be seen strange mosses and sponges, of every imaginable hue and shape, and between them bushes and creeping vines.

"This is a submarine paradise!" whispered Dave. "Did you ever dream of anything so lovely?"

"Lovely—and dangerous!" came from Amos Fearless. And then he added: "I see nothing of the *Happy Hour*."

He was right—there was no sign of a sunken ship anywhere.

"Let us take the diving bell in a grand circle around this spot," suggested Dave.

His father agreed, providing the thing could be accomplished without positive danger.

To move around, they had to pull the machine along from one tree-top to another by means of the crab-like claws attached to the bottom.

The diving bell worked like a charm and soon a distance of several hundred yards had been covered.

Sometimes the crab-like claws would slip on the tree-tops and at others the trees would break off with a dull, snapping report. When this would happen the sap flowing from the tree would be pure yellow in color.

In order to see at a great distance Amos Fearless now adjusted a powerful light which had been brought along, using a small reflector behind it.

Suddenly Dave let out a cry:

"The rival divers!"

He was right. At a great distance he had seen the other diving bell coming down.

It contained Vixen and Walton. Bart Hankers had said he was coming down with them, but had backed out at the last moment, much to the divers' satisfaction, for they had counted that he would only be in their way.

As swiftly as the other diving bell had come into view, it now faded from sight beyond another portion of the great submarine forest.

"They are close upon our heels," muttered Dave, and again Amos Fearless shook his head, doubtfully.

At last the diving bell gained the edge of the forest and came to a rest upon one of the banks of moss of many colors.

A short distance away the bank sloped downward into a sort of valley.

Here it was darker, and what there was at the bottom of the valley there was no telling without an investigation.

Should they leave the diving bell upon an exploring tour?

They debated the subject for several minutes.

It would be a risky thing to do, although as yet they had encountered no strange fish or marine monsters at this great depth.

With care they adjusted their diving suits and then armed themselves with their knives and submarine guns.

Then the door of the bell was opened slowly.

The pressure of the water became enormous and their suits of steel creaked as if to crash in upon them, as a shell can squeeze in upon the inside of an egg.

But they had calculated upon all this, and the suits held as expected.

When they stepped out upon the moss they found it as soft and yielding as a thick velvet carpet.

They advanced with caution toward the edge of the slope before them, casting their eyes continually upon all sides for the first sign of danger.

They had thus gone a distance of two hundred feet when Dave pointed to a mound to their right.

He had seen something strange moving among the moss.

Of a sudden the moss was uplifted like a blanket and the young diver fell back in amazement.

Before him stood a monster as startling as it was horrible.

Whether it was fish, beast, or demon, he could not tell, but it was certainly so awful that his very heart appeared to stop beating as he gazed upon it.

It had a long, round body, fat and blubbery, with two legs in the center, two arms near the neck, and at the end the tail of a fish.

The head was shaped like a huge pear, with eyes blinking savagely from either side of a nose which was as long and pointed as a cow's horn.

The mouth of the demon was wide open, showing a double row of sharp, bluish teeth and a tongue covered with yellow slime.

All told, the creature was at least ten feet long, and when it stood up it towered well over the heads of the two divers.

On the instant Dave raised his gun, but his father was before him, and a bullet from Amos Fearless' submarine gun took the demon squarely in the breast.

Hardly had the bullet reached its mark than the demon uttered a roar which rang in the divers' ears like thunder.

As if by magic the roar was answered from half a dozen near-by places and the moss was flung right and left.

The demons of the ocean's bottom had been sleeping, and the roar had aroused them to a sense of danger.

They came walking and swimming up from every direction, and in a twinkle Amos Fearless and Dave found themselves surrounded and hopelessly cut off from the diving bell!

CHAPTER 29

THE ESCAPE FROM THE DEMONS

It was a situation calculated to make the stoutest heart quail.

Amos Fearless and Dave were surrounded by the demons of the deep!

The horrible ocean monsters pressed close upon them, their big eyes fairly starting from their heads, their long arms working convulsively, and their sweeping tails working the brine up into a milk-white foam.

Evidently the battle-cry had gone forth, for more monsters were coming up each instant.

Father and son looked at each other mutely. Both felt that the end must be near.

The din increased, and being under water was so painful to the two divers that they almost fainted from the concussions.

In the midst of the uproar, however, there came a sudden and dead silence.

Other monsters were approaching, leading to the scene a monster larger than the rest. It was the king of the submarine demons.

At the approach of the king all the others fell back.

The king advanced, with eyes as staring as his followers, but with a tail that was motionless.

Ten feet from Amos Fearless and Dave he halted.

For a moment nothing was done upon either side.

Evidently the king of the demons was calculating the best manner of attacking the strange objects which had appeared in his realm.

He had seen the dead bodies of human beings, but never had he beheld live human beings, with skins of steel and rubber.

At last he came up cautiously and put out one long and bony hand towards Dave.

The movement was so slow that Dave was filled more with curiosity than with fear.

The king of the demons felt of Dave's legs, his body and his arms.

Then he took hold of the submarine gun and suddenly wrenched it from the young diver's grasp.

With the gun he went back to his followers.

In the meantime the demon that had been shot was slowly dying, surrounded by a number of his friends.

As soon as he was dead the others rent him limb from limb and began to eat him up!

They were cannibals!

The king of the demons handled the gun he had taken rather gingerly, nevertheless his hand, or paw, struck the trigger, and the submarine weapon was discharged full into the face of another demon sitting near.

A wild sound immediately arose, and as the shot demon fell back dead, several other demons closed in upon the king.

Soon the monsters were fighting wildly among themselves. The water was dyed half a dozen shades, shutting in the fighters as in a cloud.

Amos Fearless touched Dave on the arm and motioned his son to follow him.

The young diver understood, and in haste the pair withdrew from the circle of combat.

Then they literally ran for the diving bell.

It was a fearful strain upon each, for their diving suits weighed seventy-five pounds apiece.

They were still a score of feet from the bell when some of the demons saw them running and started in pursuit.

"We are lost now!" thought Dave, but continued to run, and urged his parent before him.

At last both gained the diving bell, all but exhausted.

Entering, they snapped the door shut and sent the signal up.

Soon the bell was rising. To assist, they began to pump the water out of the bell.

The demons swarmed all around the bell, but did not dare to touch the glass sides or the crab-like claws.

Soon the bell passed from the zone of submarine light and then the demons dropped back, for they could not breathe in the upper portions of the ocean.

The bell cleared of water, father and son took off their diving suits.

"Thank Heaven we are out of that!" came in the sign language from Amos Fearless.

"We were lucky to escape," answered Dave, earnestly. "But, father, the treasure—how will we ever get at it, with those demons around?"

At this the old diver shook his head slowly.

It was a problem difficult, if not impossible, to solve.

"I wouldn't like to meet those fellows again for a million dollars," went on Dave.

And his father agreed with him.

It seemed a long while before they emerged from the ocean, at the side of the *Swallow*.

Those on the ship lost no time in bringing them on board and questioning them regarding what they had discovered.

The story about the demons was listened to with keen interest by Doctor Barrell.

"Ah, they must belong to the lost order of chilusia damondaribytis!" cried the learned man. "They are supposed to have lived at one time upon the lost continent of Atlantis. But if so, how did they come here, in the middle of the Pacific? It is a great mystery. You must bring up one of them in the net."

"Thanks, but I don't want the job," replied Dave, quickly.

"But, my dear young man, think of the interest to science—the—the great fame it will bring you."

"Not if the chilu-what's-his-name chews me up, doctor. You just ought to see them. Why, they are enough to give you bad dreams for a month."

"Then I will go down myself in the diving bell. If it is light, as you say, perhaps I can get some snapshot photographs of them," went on the learned man.

"What if they take it into their heads to smash the diving bell to pieces?"

"Cannot you keep them at a distance with the submarine firearms?"

"Hardly; but I was thinking we might take down some submarine torpedoes," went on Dave, suddenly.

The matter was talked over for fully an hour, and at last it was decided that another trial should be made the next day, and the divers should take along two submarine torpedoes, with which to blow up the demons should the latter molest them.

In the meantime Captain Broadbeam had his glass trained upon the *Raven*, and presently he announced that the diving bell from that ship was coming up.

All watched eagerly for the reappearance of Vixen and Walton, the rival divers.

At last the men were hauled up on the deck of the *Raven*.

It was seen that Walton was injured and had to be carried to the cabin by some of the sailors.

The rival divers had met only two of the demons of the deep, but an awful conflict had occurred, and Walton had had his left arm nearly torn from the socket and was suffering from the effects of the water which had poured into his diving suit.

"I'll not go down again," announced Vixen. "Not for a thousand dollars a trip."

"What, you don't intend to give up the search already?" cried Lemuel Hankers, in horror.

"I do."

"But you agreed to find the *Happy Hour*," put in Bart. "You must stick to your agreement."

"It's wuss nor putting your head into a lion's mouth," persisted Cal Vixen. "If you don't believe it, go down yourself."

"I will go down—if you'll go with me," said Bart. He was so anxious to get the Washington fortune that his former timidity was overcome.

Vixen held out all day about going down again, but several drinks of liquor at last made him bolder, and he agreed to try once more, providing Bart would go with him, and providing the bell was stored with explosives with which to fight off the demons if they showed themselves again.

The day proved cloudy, and it looked as if a storm were brewing.

"But I don't reckon we'll get it right away," said Captain Broadbeam. "And if you want to get ahead of the *Raven's* crowd you had better go down. I see they are getting ready to put their bell over again."

At half-past nine the *Swallow's* diving bell was hoisted into the Pacific once more, and Dave and his father entered it.

"We may never see you again, captain," said the young diver. "If we don't, good-by!"

A minute later the diving bell disappeared beneath the surface of the mighty Pacific.

CHAPTER 30

IN A DIVING BELL

Down and down went the bell.

The spot chosen was about five hundred feet to the northward of where the bell had gone down before—directly over the valley the divers had discovered.

Amos Fearless was of the opinion that if the *Happy Hour* was at all in that vicinity she must lie at the bottom of the valley.

The dark zone of waters was passed, and now they came into the light once more.

The water was warm and as clear as crystal, showing nothing of the dye and foam produced by the battle of the deep-sea monsters.

A number of curious fish sailed past the diving bell—fish which they had not seen before.

One was jet-black and shaped exactly like a pillow tied in the middle.

Another was red, white, and blue, with six eyes which shone like stars of silver.

"That's a regular starry-flag fish," was Dave's comment. "I wonder if we can take the sight of that for a good sign?"

"Let us hope so," answered Amos Fearless, in his sign language.

The old diver's voice was gradually improving, and that morning he had spoken a few words to Dave in a hoarse whisper.

At last they came in sight of that mossy plain, which, the day before, had almost been the scene of their death.

The diving bell was halted and they gazed around sharply for some sign of the demons.

Not a monster of the deep was in sight.

The moss was torn up on all sides, and here and there lay parts of bodies and bones, but that was all.

"Perhaps they all killed each other," suggested Dave.

"Let us hope so," came from his father.

The mossy plain was now passed, and gradually the diving bell slipped down the slope of the valley beyond.

Here the light was not so good and they had to turn on the electricity.

At the bottom of the valley grew a number of submarine trees and bushes, with vines which sent up their swaying bodies several hundreds of feet into the crystal-like water.

At last the diving bell came to a stop at the very bottom of the valley, among the trees.

They signaled to stop lowering and then brought out a tiny searchlight which had been brought along.

This was swept in every direction.

Suddenly Dave uttered an exclamation:

"Look! There is something which resembles a ship's stern!"

The young diver was right. Far down the valley his eye had beheld some woodwork, half buried in the muck and moss.

In a few minutes both father and son were working the claw-like feet of the diving bell and moving toward the wreckage in crab-like fashion.

As they advanced they saw a dark object above them coming down swiftly.

Amos Fearless caught his son by the arm and both drew back.

Then Dave gave a start.

The dark object was the diving bell from the *Raven*!

The bell contained Cal Vixen, Lemuel Hankers, and Bart.

Dave motioned to his father in the sign language of the divers:

"Come, let us get to the wreck first."

Amos Fearless caught his son by the arm and moved forward once more.

But the rival diving bell was between them and their object, and they had to make a semicircle with their own diving bell.

The rivals now saw the bell from the *Swallow*, and as both bells came closer, Lemuel Hankers shook his fist at the Fearlesses.

"You're a cheerful enemy," was Dave's dry comment.

Soon our friends were close to the wreckage, and Dave gave a shout:

"The *Happy Hour*! See, the name is on the stern!"

He was right, the wreck was indeed that of the ship for which they had searched so long.

The second diving bell now came up and came to a standstill directly at the side of the wreck.

But Dave was the first on board, and as Vixen approached he motioned to the rival diver in the sign language:

"We claim this wreck, which we discovered first."

"We claim the wreck," returned Cal Vixen.

And he made several motions to Lemuel Hankers and his son.

It soon looked as if there would be a fight then and there, but this would have been suicidal for all hands.

Yet when Dave and his father tried to enter the cabin of the *Happy Hour*, Cal Vixen attempted to bar their way.

Instantly Amos Fearless seized the rival diver and hurled him back.

"Touch me or my son and you will pay dearly for it," he motioned to Vixen.

At this the rival diver fell back, knowing full well that Amos Fearless was not a person with whom to trifle.

Slowly and cautiously Dave entered the cabin of the *Happy Hour*.

His father followed, and at a respectable distance came Cal Vixen and the two Hankers.

The cabin was badly wrecked, and in it nothing of value remained.

"I wonder if we can get down into the hold," thought Dave, and motioned to his father.

"We will try," came back from the old diver. "But be careful, or you won't get out alive."

The pair advanced with great caution, going down through the forward hatch.

In the meantime the rival party entered the hold by the rear hatch.

It was very dark, and the electric light shone but dimly here, for the water was so foul it contaminated the air they carried.

To the intense surprise of all, the hold of the *Happy Hour* was absolutely bare!

Dave could scarcely believe the evidence of his senses.

The great treasure was gone!

Their trip to the middle of the Pacific and to the bottom of that mighty ocean had availed them nothing.

Father and son stared helplessly at each other and then at the rival party.

All were equally dumfounded.

The rage of the Hankers knew no bounds.

Lemuel Hankers would not believe the truth, and had Cal Vixen go with him and Bart on a thorough search throughout the wreck, and all around it.

It was useless; the *Happy Hour* and the vicinity were absolutely bare of the first trace of gold, or, in fact, of anything of value.

With heavy hearts the Hankers party returned to their diving bell.

"The jig is up!" cried Bart, as soon as he was inside and could speak. "Oh, what a sell!"

"I was mad to believe in it!" came from Lemuel Hankers. "And to think that I have spent thousands of dollars on a fool's errand!" And tears of miserly rage flowed down his cheeks.

"I reckon we might as well go up," put in Cal Vixen. He, too, was disgusted.

They gave the signal, and gradually their diving bell began to leave the valley at the ocean's bottom.

But less than quarter of a mile of the distance to the surface was covered when there came a shock on top of the diving bell which sent all inside sprawling headlong.

Then came another shock and the water began to pour into the bell.

Some great monster of the deep had hit the bell and cracked some of the upper joints.

The collision showed those above that something was wrong, and they began to haul in faster than ever.

But great damage had been done also to the monster, which was somewhat similar to a deep-sea whale.

He became entangled in the guide line of the diving bell and was hauled up to the surface in spite of himself.

"Hullo, what's this?" cried Captain Nesik, when the monster came into view.

Then ensued a battle royal for fully five minutes.

At last the monster was cut loose and disappeared, with a loud splash, into the ocean.

Then the diving bell was hoisted aboard and opened.

It was found that those inside had been almost drowned, and all were unable to help themselves and had to be carried to the ship's cabin. Here they lingered for many hours between life and death.

The diving bell was ruined, and it was doubtful if another search for the treasure could be made by the Hankers' party.

CHAPTER 31

THE TREASURE AT LAST—CONCLUSION

Little dreaming of the accident which had overtaken their rivals, Amos Fearless and Dave returned to their own diving bell.

The heart of each was heavy, and for several minutes neither felt like speaking.

"A wild-goose chase," said the old diver at last. "I might have known it would prove so."

"But what has become of the gold?" returned Dave. "It couldn't walk off of itself."

"That is true. Perhaps those on board of the *Happy Hour* took it off, when they found the ship was about to sink."

"But they never brought any of the treasure to land."

"No—at least, none that was reported. They might have done such a thing in secret."

"Supposing we move the bell around and make another search," suggested Dave. "The demons appear to have vanished."

They pumped in a fresh supply of air and then moved around in a large circle.

It was hard work, and the confinement of the diving bell gave each a headache and a strange ringing in the ears.

Presently they came to a curiously shaped mound of shells, covered with moss.

"Hullo, what's this?" said Dave. "Hang me if it doesn't look like the home of some submarine animal. Perhaps it's a meeting house for those demons."

"If it is, we had better move on," replied Amos Fearless, in the sign language.

But Dave was curious to investigate, and presently they replaced their helmets, took in some fresh air, and sallied forth to examine the mound.

Inside all was damp—a dampness different from that produced by the water around them.

The mound proved to be hollow, with the walls covered with brilliant seashells of all colors.

At the top was a round hole to admit light.

In the center was a smaller mound, with a curious hump in the middle.

"Nothing here," signed Amos Fearless, when of a sudden something glittering caught Dave's eye.

He stooped and picked up—a gold coin!

In a moment he was digging away at the small mound in the center of the shell-like structure.

The moss came away readily, and to their gaze was disclosed—a heap of shining gold!

"The treasure!" burst from the young diver. "Found at last!"

His father was equally pleased.

The gold was mixed with bits of other bright metal and glass, for whoever had stored it there had known no difference in value and had simply made a collection of stuff bright to the eye.

"Let us go back and fill up the diving bell," said Amos Fearless, by signs.

Dave was more than willing, and they soon had the diving bell as close as possible to the door of the mound.

They had brought several bags along, and into these they began heaping the gold.

It was hard work, but this they did not mind.

The finding of the treasure meant to them a lifetime of leisure, had they a mind to take it.

At last the bags were full and still more of the gold remained.

"We will pile it on the floor of the diving bell," signed Amos Fearless. "Let us make one trip of it. After this I never wish to visit the bottom of the sea again."

Both worked steadily, and in half an hour had every piece of gold in sight picked up.

They were just taking the last of the gold to the diving bell when a horrible roar broke upon their ears.

The demons of the deep were returning to the locality.

"Quick!" cried Dave. "Or it will be all up with us!"

Father and son ran for the diving bell.

But now the demons saw them and the roar increased.

Soon fully fifty of the ferocious creatures were leaping and swimming toward the mound.

Their sharp teeth clicked together as if anxious to bury themselves in the bodies of the human beings.

With all haste Amos Fearless and Dave got into the diving bell. But before they could close the door one of the demons was upon them.

He caught the old diver by the head, intending to pull that member from the rest of the body.

Dave's heart leaped into his throat, yet his presence of mind did not desert him.

Raising one of the submarine guns he blazed away and caught the monster of the deep straight in the mouth and throat.

Mortally wounded, the demon fell back, one arm still within the doorway of the diving bell.

As quickly as possible Amos Fearless turned and shoved the arm outside.

Dave was about to close the door when his father motioned him to desist.

Then the old diver caught up one of the torpedoes which had been brought along, set its clock-like movements in motion, and hurled it forth among the approaching company of demons.

It fell in their midst, and, attracted by the shining metallic covering of the torpedo, all crowded around the object.

As they did this, the door of the diving bell was closed and the signal was sent up to hoist away immediately.

Hardly had the diving bell begun to move when a fearful shock made it quiver from top to bottom and cracked one of the glass sides.

The torpedo had exploded, dealing death and destruction among the demons of the deep, impossible to describe.

Fully a score of the monsters were utterly annihilated, while nearly every one of the others was badly wounded.

One that escaped came after the diving bell, trying vainly to destroy the bell and those inside.

But an unlucky movement caused the demon to come in contact with one of the crab-like claws of the bell, and seeing this, Dave worked the claw instantly, thus making the demon a prisoner.

The creature flopped violently, but as the bell ascended to the upper waters of the ocean, it seemed to become stunned, and before the surface was gained it lay utterly helpless.

Soon the diving bell was hoisted aboard of the *Swallow*.

"The gold at last!" cried Captain Broadbeam. "Hurrah! I was afraid something awful had happened."

"And the wonderful monster," put in Doctor Barrell. "What an odd creature! It will make a grand exhibition at the Smithsonian Institution."

"You'll have to pickle him in alcohol, doctor," said Dave, with a laugh.

Both Amos Fearless and Dave were very weak from having remained at the ocean's bottom so long, and it was several days before either felt entirely like himself again.

Strange to say, however, the trip after the treasure had helped Mr. Fearless' organs of speech, and soon he could talk almost as well as ever.

"This is the best yet," declared Dave. "It's better than finding the treasure."

"I am thankful from the bottom of my heart," answered the old diver, and his face showed that he spoke the truth.

"I don't think that I want to go to the bottom of the Pacific again, father."

"Nor I, Dave. It is too full of perils."

The storm that had been threatening broke the next day, and was a great strain on the *Swallow* and likewise on the *Raven*. The latter ship sprung a leak, and the *Swallow* stood by, ready to offer assistance if she should go down.

During that time those on the *Raven* heard of the finding of the treasure.

"I claim half of that treasure," said Lemuel Hankers.

"You'll never get it," replied Amos Fearless, firmly.

When the two ships separated it was discovered by those on the *Swallow* that Pete Rackley was missing.

"Do you know what I think?" said Dave. "I think he escaped to the *Raven*."

"Well, let him go," said Captain Broadbeam. "We can well afford to do without him."

"Do you think the Hankers will make any further trouble for us?" asked Dave of his father.

"That remains to be seen," answered Amos Fearless. The Hankers and their friends did try to make trouble, and how will be told in another volume, to be called "The Cruise of the Treasure Ship; or, The Castaways of Floating Island."

After the storm the weather cleared off nicely, and then Captain Broadbeam lost no time in beginning the long journey to San Francisco.

"I suppose you want to bank that gold as soon as possible," he said to Amos Fearless.

"Yes, I shall not feel safe about it until it is stored in some bank vault," was the answer.

"And father and I intend to give all on board of this ship their just share of the treasure," put in Dave.

"Well, I shan't complain of that," returned Captain Broadbeam, with a smile. "You've got a big pile and no mistake."

"Won't the folks at home stare when they hear the news!" said Dave to his father. "Why, we'll have enough money to buy half of the town, and more."

"I shall be glad of one thing, Dave."

"You want to give up diving?"

"Yes, I feel that I am getting too old for the work. Besides, I am afraid of losing my power of speech again."

"Then give it up by all means, father." And the youth gave his parent a hug which meant a great deal.

The outlook was very bright for both father and son; and here we will leave them, knowing that neither will ever forget the day when he met the rival divers and went down to the bottom of the Pacific for the sunken treasure.